To

Mrs Cle

Enjoy reading !

Best Wishes

About the Author

D. Oudit is a British author of Trinidadian heritage. He grew up in a large family, experiencing privilege as well as poverty. As a surgeon for more than twenty years, he has practised in various contrasting environments, each with their own individual emotional challenges. He has been a first-hand witness to a wide range of expressions of human emotions played out in real life, from the sparkle in the eyes of a newborn to the desperate plea of the dying on their last breath — and all the shades of grey in between. He captures some of this in his tale.

A World for The Others

D. Oudit

A World for The Others
An Inspiring Tale of Life, Fate and Destiny

Olympia Publishers
London

www.olympiapublishers.com
OLYMPIA PAPERBACK EDITION

A CIP catalogue record for this title is
available from the British Library.

ISBN: 978-1-80074-223-9

This is a work of fiction.
Names, characters, places and incidents originate from the writer's
imagination. Any resemblance to actual persons, living or dead, is
purely coincidental.

First Published in 2022

Olympia Publishers
Tallis House
2 Tallis Street
London
EC4Y 0AB

Printed in Great Britain

Dedication

This book is dedicated to my late parents.
Every bit of pride they had in me gave me the strength and
courage to be a better person.

Acknowledgements

I wish to sincerely acknowledge my loving and beautiful wife, Michelle, for believing in and supporting me throughout. None of this would have possible without her love. I would also like to thank my daughter, Chelsea, for being a true angel in our lives.

Prologue

'Sheer will and determination are one's only weapons against karma'

Life is like a trying to get a bag-full of marbles into a jar. For some, the jar is large, for others it is small. Although all jars are meant to be seen as equal, large jars fill much more easily than smaller ones. Despite this and even though it may not be as easy to do so, small jars could be filled too. And this is what is most important to realise. Now, how we go about achieving this is interesting. Some would meticulously pick up individual marbles from the bag and safely transfer them to the jar. On the other hand, others would be more adventurous throw the lot up into the air and wait to see how many would find themselves inside the jar. Yet still, many may even not even bother with the marbles in the bag to fill the jar, and choose instead to use the first substitute that attracts their attention — preferably shiny ones. After all, they must be the better ones as marbles are not even shiny! So, which is the correct way? Does it matter? Maybe it is really about how filled your jar is at the end that counts. Maybe that's all it is about! Maybe it is that simple, or is it really?

Seated at the front row of an almost empty, modern concert hall in the heart of Los Angeles, was an elderly gentleman of a long-expired generation. Although he appeared seemingly frail, his physical appearance was propped up by the events of a memorable life and the strength of his achievements, many of which were mostly forgotten by the world and the people around. The atmosphere in the great hall was as light as air. The perfect milieu for reflection and contemplation of a life, filled with fortune and misfortune, aspirations and hardships, accomplishments and disappointments and success and failure.

After a long time, Robert Lancaster had been given an offer to attend a concert featuring, arguably, the best orchestra in the world. As he sat on the front row of a soon-to-be filled-to capacity concert hall, he realised that he had fifteen minutes of quiet time before the doors opened to the other patrons. He sat there, and with deep breaths in, savoured the moment of quietness and peace, as his escorts left through the very doors he had entered moments before in his wheelchair.

One of the greatest luxuries in life was dabbling in a bit of solace and reflection in a quiet atmosphere, he thought to himself. He could remember the very first time he attended this glorious hall as a youngster, barely affording the entrance fee.

"Oh, how much time has passed; how much have changed," he thought to himself. "Am I any happier today, than I was as a kid, some seventy years ago?" he asked himself.

Despite the feeling that he really did not have much to show for this physically, he felt roundly proud to admit that he never was a passive passenger in his journey through life. Although he thought to himself that his life, on reflection, may appear very much like a car crash, he felt vindicated with the knowledge that he had embraced every challenge with all his might and abilities, in a warm and loving manner.

After all, he thought, "I could not bear to emerge on the other side of life without making, not just a difference, but a positive one! I just wanted the world to be better place for hosting me here in my lifetime."

He had done so much in his life, conquered many a fear, but what stood out most to him, over the entirety of his lifetime, was his achievement of acquiring the love of people, one by one. This, he recalled, was his greatest success of all!

Creaking sounds filled the air, followed almost instantaneously by the blurred noises of patrons with a melody of its own, one of excitement! If there was any will to prevent it, it would have certainly been futile. The noises grew from low murmurs to thunderous echoes, like the hulk of a sinking ship losing its battle with the forces of the ocean. The tiny discrete worlds of people, friends and families all coalescing into the single universe of a concert hall, allowing themselves to share one common love that evening.

As the noise died, the curtains opened leaving no expectation unfulfilled...

Chapter 1
Dances with Love

Love is the force that melts away the shells of souls, allowing all to merge into one

Robert had an unwavering love for music which he developed an early age. It was like a sanctuary to escape the stresses of everyday life and experience unfathomable peace. It was one of the great attributes which attracted him to his wife. But unlike her, he was not musically gifted. He made many attempts in his lifetime to learn to play various musical instruments from the piano, violin and cello to the saxophone. Any degree of success was probably akin to a pinch of dust in a vast desert of expectations. But nevertheless, it was the language of music that consoled his soul.

He was twenty years old when he met Margot, the love of his life. She was a talented violinist whose love for the world was immeasurable. That afternoon, she was playing in a string quartet at the Christmas fair for a local charity organisation. As Robert joined the dynamic audience on the pedestrianised street in the heart of Los Angeles, her music captivated his attention. But more so, his first glance at the stunningly beautiful, young violinist, stole his heart.

The crowd of spectators surrounding the quartet was ever changing in composition; as folks arrived, others left to get on with their mundane activities. The only single constant there, that afternoon, was the young mesmerised Robert, who stood there unwaveringly, for three hours, without as much a single movement, just breathing with excitement. He enjoyed the music on offer at the time, but more importantly, he developed more of an interest in the young violinist whose exquisite beauty was enhanced by and communicated through her flawless musical prowess. Oh, how he wished he could let her know how beautiful she was or even, maybe ask her out. But the young Robert was too shy at the time. He did not have the confidence to approach her.

He waited until the end of the concert before he left. He managed to do so with a heavy heart and a longing to see her again. Following that day, he visited that very spot every evening and every weekend to see whether she was there, but was not that lucky or fated. This bugged him subconsciously for weeks afterwards. "If only I had the courage to say 'hello' even, when I had a chance to," he thought.

The month after, Robert finally had a pay check after taking up a role in a computer company. Although he loved music passionately — so much that he did not need an excuse to attend a musical concert — he never did have the opportunity to attend a concert in a formal concert hall. Every time he passed by the Hollywood Bowl; he would imagine the day he could afford a ticket to attend a concert there. Well now, he had managed to save enough to afford this little luxury. A treat to himself.

Dressed in his finest suit, he went along to the Hollywood Bowl. As the concert started, he sat back on his seat in preparation to allow the music to percolate through the fabric of his being. At that point, he looked up and was pleasantly surprised. He thought that he could recognise the violinist at the front row of the orchestral line up.

Robert pinched himself to make sure that he was not just seeing what his subconscious mind wanted him to. He sat upright most attentively, and his eyes never once lost contact with the beautiful, young violinist throughout the duration of the concert. Whilst his evening was spent like this in the concert hall, his inner energy was divided between his attraction to the violinist and summoning the courage to speak to her that evening, if the opportunity presented itself, despite the great and unimaginable odds. His soul was restless. He had to… he just had to speak to her.

At the end of the concert, he managed to sneak past the security guard and entered the backstage hall, where the beautiful young violinist appeared to be standing all alone. Although this seemed like an opportunity for him to approach her, he was over-actively nervous. However, there was some sort of strong, mystical attractive force emanating directly from his heart that evening. It was hard to ignore or subdue. This was the source of his subconscious troubles over the last few months. It was a phenomenon he could not quite understand completely, nor explain satisfactorily.

As he mustered up a magnitude of courage of herculean proportion, he approached the young violinist.

'The music was lovely; I love the way you play the violin…so gracefully. It is inspiring,' he said to the young lady.

She looked up, flashed a warm smile at him and responded, 'Well, thank you so much.'

Robert introduced himself to her, 'Hi, I am Robert Lancaster.'

She reciprocated, 'Hi, I am Margot Walters.'

As their eyes caught each other, the magic that was generated was enough to ignite an eternity of boundless love between them.

'So, are you interested in music, Robert?' asked Margot.

'Of course, it fuels my soul,' he replied. 'But I wish I was the slightest bit talented at playing, though. I have tried many instruments that I love, but you know, they never loved me back. Just never had the talent.'

They both chuckled amorously.

'You know, you don't have to know how to play music, if you are not good at it, to enjoy it,' Margot quipped teasingly.

'I know, but it has never stopped me from trying,' said Robert.

He then invited her for a cup of coffee at a nearby café where they sat and shared a conversation. They spent hours talking about topic after topic. This spark of magic blossomed into a date and then several more afterwards. They fell madly in love with each other. They did not then need another excuse to spend every free moment they had together, relishing each other's company. Their common love for music formed a herculean bond between them that catalysed their endless love for each other.

They frequented musical concerts together and Robert never missed any of Margot's performances. As their relationship effortlessly blossomed over time, they found more and more excuses to spend time with each other. They shared the things that mattered in life and which they both valued, a healthy love for each other, wonderful experiences, trust and honesty.

Later that year, a week before Thanksgiving, Margot invited Robert to accompany her to her parents' home in San

Francisco. Robert was immediately excited about the prospect of spending the day with Margot and meeting her parents.

Upon arriving there, they were greeted by Margot's mom and dad. They lived in a considerably large house, hidden from the rest of world in a beautifully scenic countryside town. The house was accessible through a long winding driveway lined by beautiful trees, and was surrounded by a happy and beautiful garden.

Margot's parents were both retired magistrates and academics. The retired couple did not offer Robert the warm welcome he was hoping for. This was indeed uncomfortable and quite disappointing for him. He found that there was very little that they could converse about as there were few topics of common interest. It was noticeably awkward being in their company.

"It is funny how different folks could be, hmm," Robert thought to himself as they sat around the dinner table.

Although, there was a world of commonalities between Margot and himself, it was obvious that he was struggling to fit into her parents' world. This became even more uncomfortably obvious as the afternoon passed. Soon, the silence sounded louder in the room they shared. Then suddenly, this changed. Mr Walters reluctantly grasped the initiative to speak to Robert.

'So where are you from? Tell me a bit about yourself?'

'I am from LA, was born in New York and...' began Robert, when he was suddenly interrupted by his host.

'What do you do... for a living I mean?' he asked.

Robert promptly replied that he was working for a computer company and that he had previously worked for a local newspaper firm. But before he could continue, he was interrupted yet again by a string of questions in close succession.

'Are you a journalist, then? Where did you go to university? What are your career plans?' Mr Walters asked.

Robert was at first taken aback by the verbal ambush, but not at all surprised. It fitted perfectly with the mood of the room.

He took a moment before replying, 'No, I am not a journalist, I'm not so sure at this stage what my definitive career plans are, but all I know is that I want to end up doing something I love, something I could commit to and work hard at.'

'Surely you must have some sort of an idea? What did you major in at university?' Mr Walters thundered.

'I did not graduate from university, sir,' he quietly, but firmly replied.

'Hmmmm, I see... I see,' replied the gentleman in a deflated but yet quietly, victorious tone, almost affirming the point he wanted he bring out, much like a lawyer cross-examining a witness on the stand.

Mrs Walters then took up the baton to, not so subtly, point out that their daughter graduated at the top of her class from Stanford University.

'Margot is talented and has so much potential,' she added.

'She is not only the cleverest person I know, but has the warmest heart and that speaks through her beautiful music,' responded Robert.

Both parents nodded in agreement as they looked up at her, not with a stare of admiration but one of disappointment, at that moment in time.

After dinner, Margot and Robert were led to the living room. Mrs Walters went off to the kitchen and her husband invited Robert to have a seat on the sofa. He then asked if he could have a word in private with Margot in his study and she agreed as they both went off through the large panel-glass double-doors.

Robert found himself alone in the living room. His eyes gazed at the wooden panels on the walls and the photographs of aristocratic figures on the walls, all neatly arranged. It was symbolic of a highly successful family over many generations. The strange thing was, none of this felt like the warmth that glows from Margot. She seemed truly different.

Mr Walters led Margot to his study, a place where as a young child, she was not allowed to enter unless accompanied by himself. Nothing looked any different in there now than ten or fifteen years ago, despite the caress of time. Although, it appeared aristocratic and of expensive taste, it did not have exude warmth. It conveyed an almost wooden, monotonous character.

Margot was motioned to have a seat on the sofa as Mr Walters paced restlessly towards the high window overlooking the well-manicured gardens.

Facing the window, he began, 'I speak for both your mother and I. It is indeed lovely to see you again. Thank you for joining us.'

His tone and mannerism were quite cold, as if he was setting the stage for an uncomfortable conversation.

There was a long pause before Margot replied, 'I am happy to be here and so is Robert.'

'Hmmm, I was hoping we could have a chat about him, if that was all right,' her dad stated, rather firmly.

Margot, knowing how the conversation was likely to be directed, decided to pre-empt the awkwardness by attempting to describe the wonderful person that Robert was and that she had now, undoubtedly, developed a close emotional bond towards.

'Robert is a very caring person; he has a good heart,' she began before being interrupted.

'How long have you known him? How much do you know about him?' her dad enquired in a dissenting tone of voice.

But before she could answer, the interrogative questions continued spewing.

'Do you think that he is the best person for you?' her dad asked.

This final question confirmed the headline of this awkward, privately held conversation. She was quite taken aback by it. The sharpness of his attacked was profound. But deep inside, she was not completely surprised.

'I have known Robert for six months. In that time, I have discovered what a wonderfully kind, humble, determined and caring person he is. Do not just judge the book by the cover and do not even try to judge him after meeting him for just under a few moments,' complained Margot.

'Margot, darling', said her father, 'I know this maybe awkward for the both of us, but I will get to the point here,' he muttered, becoming a bit impatient with his now grown-up daughter. 'I think you have had enough time to notice that that guy has no future. He is a loser, he doesn't even come from a worthwhile background!' he thundered. 'You, on the other hand, are from such an elite background; you have had one of best educations possible and you have a bright future. Why the hell are going to waste all of that on a loser like him?'

By then, Margot was utterly disgusted by the conversation. 'I am an adult and I am well capable of making a sensible decision on my own. I wish you would believe in me a bit more, rather than adopt an intangible and questionable attitude that has been the backbone of the custom of this family for far too long!' she defensively replied, with tears in her eyes.

Following more than a moment of deafening silence, allowing some time for calming of the high tensions in the room that afternoon, there was clear evidence of a failure to normalise to a middle ground between the opposing strong points of view between both of them.

'Your mother and I agree that you should terminate this relationship at once!' Mr Walters ordered in the low, firm tone of voice of a magistrate barking an order from his throne in the courtroom.

This was met with a quick opposing and equal response from Margot.

'I am sorry you both feel that way, but at this moment in time, Robert feels like the right one for me! More importantly though, I am not going to let my life dictated by you and your archaic values. I will make own decisions!' she declared.

The old man was clearly not prepared for, or impressed with her firm stance. Neither was he used to nor prepared to be challenged.

'Then, if this is your final position on this matter, then you must stand alone, on your own,' he said, after taking a deep breath.

When she heard this, it felt like a bullet ricocheting straight through her heart. She could not stand to expect or accept this from her father, amongst all people. She stood there, in front of the tall greyed man, frozen, not quite knowing how to process this insult. Her emotions and her entire existence were overtaken by such a shock that her body went into "safe-mode" to survive the moments which were to follow. She felt the life-long love and admiration she had for her parents almost completely slipping away from her soul through the tears rolling down her cheeks. Her life had changed forever, in that instant.

After her father left the room, she took a few moments to compose herself and returned to the living room. There, she found Robert, sitting with her mom and dad in an emotionally dead room. Each had a cup of hot herb tea, in unmarked cups with no character. She found that there was one ready for her as she walked over to take her place.

After several awkward moments of silence, Mrs Walters asked Robert, 'So tell me, what is it that you like about music?' Robert took a moment to compose his thoughts before replying.

'Music does not have the same meaning to everyone. Some folks can feel it in their insides and the reason for that is inexplicable. But more importantly, is what it does to me,' he calmly replied. 'It stirs the juices in my soul to make what is unpleasant in there, bearable if not, enjoyable, and what is pleasant, ecstatic.' He continued before his answer was interrupted by silence which seemed to be all too abundant in that house.

'How much of that feeling you experience is dependent on how much is afforded to you by the musician. A great musician gives generously, so that the receptive souls revel in emotions. It's like a dance between the musician and listener,' he added, 'For me, that's why I love listening to Margot's music, above all else. Her music gives very generously.'

Margot realised that, in addition to this being a kind compliment, it was about how Robert, without being asked, related his love for her. The others in room may have missed this.

"We hear only that which we wish to," she thought to herself.

After tea, the young couple bade farewell to their hosts for the final time and they headed on their journey back home. Margot was quite angry but did quite well to conceal this. She believed in Robert totally. He was different from the other guys she knew. He belonged to a far different world, a much better one. It was unfortunate that her parents were not willing to see that or give him a fair chance. Although the pain she harnessed that day was unlikely to be eliminated easily, she did her best to repress it.

Chapter 2
Dances with Loss

Although life is like a wave of peak and troughs, there is purpose at every turn

Robert was born to wealthy, successful parents. They were both top lawyers in Manhattan, New York and were well into their forties when they settled down and got married. Both of them were well-driven, career-minded individuals who were at the top in their fields. Despite trying for a couple of years, they found it difficult to conceive and had given up any hopes of peering into the eyes of a little person, generated from the perfect combination of their genetic architecture.

One day, while at a deposition hearing for a case in which she was representing the mayor of New York City, Lucy, Robert's mother to-be, found it quite challenging to continue as she felt unusually sick and had to excuse herself for several moments. This unusual feeling persisted for several days before she visited the doctor. Her life lit up in an unimaginable way when she was told that she was pregnant.

Lucy's first inclination was to phone her husband, Robert, to spill the beans but decided to wait for the right moment. That evening she invited her husband to dinner at a restaurant that was quite special for them both — it was where Robert Sr.

had proposed to her five years back. She booked a table in a quiet corner of the restaurant.

She could not wait until after dinner to share the great news with her husband. As soon as he sat down, she told him, as she was admittedly powerless to be able to refrain for even moment more. Her husband was radiantly beaming on learning of this. He leapt off his seat and rushed over to her to hug her stiflingly tight.

'I can't believe my ears!' he said, as he simultaneously pinched himself.

'This is the miracle we so longed for,' screamed Lucy.

They immediately began making plans for the baby. On their way home that evening, as they walked past a shop, they both stopped and peered into the window, lovingly admiring the beautiful clothes perfectly tailored for little ones. That evening their lives had changed so much. They were truly, the happiest couple in existence, in every way imaginable.

Time flew by rather quickly, as evidence by the seemingly growing protuberance of Lucy's tummy. But still, this wasn't as fast enough for the hyper-excited couple who were expecting their 'miracle'. All preparations were done. The nursery was decorated by the couple themselves, who were surviving on the ecstasy of expectation. They just would not have it any other way. They selfishly wanted to squeeze every moment of joy out of this miraculous, but surreal, period of time. They had longed for this for far too long.

When the baby finally came, it was euphoric for them both. Robert took him in his hands and warmly looked at him, welcoming him to the world. A sadness briefly overwhelmed him when he thought how special this would have been had his parents been alive to see and hold their grandson.

Interestingly, Lucy felt the same. They both no longer had any living relatives, but were blessed with many great friends.

'Thank you so much for this blessing, thank you for coming to us. We are going to look after you with all of our lives,' Robert Sr. whispered to his newborn.

He was soon overwhelmed when the baby gently grabbed hold of his finger and directed it straight into his mouth and gently sucked on it.

'The baby must be hungry,' pointed out a nurse.

She came over to Robert and gently took the little one away to his mom to be breastfed. The next day, both mom and baby were discharged and taken home by Robert. That evening, they entered their luxury Manhattan flat for the first time, as a complete family. A scene they had always imagined and an experience they always prayed for. They named him Robert Lancaster Jr.

The following years were the most wonderful for the couple, as they lived their lives on the inside of a miracle. They spent every opportunity they could with their beloved son and relished every moment of it. Their lives were very much different now, from ever before. Their lives were more dimensional and they could not have been any happier.

The baby, Robert Jr., grew up to be an adoringly cute infant who attracted the affection of passers-by everywhere. At the age of four, they enrolled him into the most prestigious private school in the city where he was also adored by everyone. He was just starting to express a personality of his own, which was even more precious to witness.

One Friday evening, as the week drew to an end, Robert Sr. picked up Lucy from her office and was travelling along the freeway towards the school to pick up the infant. The roads were quite busy, as was expected at that time of the week. Robert Sr. was trying his best to avoid being late. His journey was not helped by the awful weather, as the heavens protested with heavy snowfall. Unfortunately, the conditions being right for it, tragedy struck.

The vehicle in front of theirs lost its grip with the road and swerved uncontrollably from left to right and vice versa. Robert stepped heavily on the brakes while he attempted to control the direction of his now vertiginously meandering car. The probability for disaster was uncontrollably high.

A loud thump, a feeling of floating away, helplessness to save his beloved wife, all overwhelmed him simultaneously. Panic, flashing lights, adrenaline-fuelled conversations and screams filled the ever-contracting space. Then, everything faded away into obscure nothingness. Existence melted away from him.

Ms Johnson who was looking after the last of the kids at the school, began pacing up down the classroom, as she really did not wish to be late for her date with a young gentleman she had only recently met, a couple weeks ago. Things were looked promising for the young couple, in a romantic way. She was keen to get there on time that evening. She looked up at the clock on the wall. It was six p.m. Robert was now the only infant to be collected.

Time went by rather painfully slow. She kept looking at the clock on the wall but the hands seemed to barely move at all. It was not unlike Robert's parents to be inconsiderate in arriving late like this, but she realised that this was not an unknown phenomenon in her experience, especially on a Friday evening. Despite this, Ms Johnson was now becoming impatient but calmed herself down as she realised that she was not going to make it in time for her date. She phoned her boyfriend and informed him that she was going to be unavoidably late that evening and that he should cancel the reservation. She requested that they find somewhere else to eat that evening, when she eventually was able to leave work.

Meanwhile, the little Robert was himself was growing impatient and becoming unsettled. She took him over to the reception room and sat with him on the sofa which was overlooked by a large wall-mounted television. She looked on at the seven o'clock news while trying to comfort the infant. The stories flicked by; a war in some part of the world, a terrible accident on the freeway with a number of deaths, a protest march on the other side of the country, a...

Her attention to the television was interrupted by noticing that the time on the clock was 7.03 p.m. She was sure Robert's parents would walk-in any second now.

Before the thought could vanish from Mrs Johnson's mind, she heard the buzzing of the intercom at the front door.

"Have they forgotten the PIN code to get in?" she wondered.

She walked testily over to the door and opened it as quickly and forcefully as she could. Her jaw dropped in shock as she found two fully-cladded policemen standing before her. Obviously, something was not quite right.

'Good evening, ma'am!' said on taller of two in a stentorian voice.

'Good evening, officers. How may I help you?' she replied.

'May we speak to the school principal, please?' replied the other policeman.

'The principal has left for the day. I am the only one here. I am waiting for the parents of the last infant to be pick him up,' replied Mrs Johnson.

'Ms...?' probingly began one of the officers.

'Johnson, Ms Johnson,' she filled in.

'Ms Johnson, may we come in please?' the officer asked.

'Sure, is there a problem?' she enquired in tremulous voice.

She directed the law enforcement men to enter and offered them a seat on the sofa. Meanwhile, Robert was running around oblivious to the verbal orders to stop. After all, school time was all over for him.

'Cute little one, what is his name?' the officer asked.

'Robert.'

'Robert Lancaster?' he questioned.

"Yes, how did you know—' she began, before she was interrupted by a nod from one of the men.

'Is there somewhere we could talk in private?' he asked, while his colleague exited the room to make a phone call.

She directed him to the other side of the hall from where Robert was happily playing.

'I am sorry, I have terrible news for you. Robert's parents' have been in a fatal car crash in the last hour or so.'

Ms Johnson's eyes swelled up with tears as her psyche almost visibly retracted into a tiny dot. She clenched her hands and sank uncontrollably into a squatting position as her legs could not find the strength to support the rest of her body. The police officer grabbed hold of her arm and controlled her descent onto the floor. His partner by then had returned from the other room and turned his attention on the clueless infant, as he ran happily around room with untampered innocence.

At this single moment in time, Robert's life changed quite dramatically. Little did he know about it, at that instant, or by how much. It was not long after he would realise it though. But little did he know, as dramatic as this life changing moment was for him, this was not going to be his last.

Chapter 3
Dances with a New Life

*Life is the greatest teacher, through its various experiences —
the good, the bad and the ugly ones*

The fate of a child, born into what many would regard as a perfect family, changed in the fraction of a moment. Nothing in life should be taken for granted. Life, guided by fate, has mysterious ways of dramatically changing, when least expected. Sometimes, for the better and sometimes, for the worse. Life consistently never follows a straight line. At every turn there are new experiences to be had and new challenges to face.

Following the loss of his world, as he had come to know it, in the relatively short space of time in which it existed, everything changed dramatically. The infant was taken to an orphanage where he spent the most significant years of his childhood. For him, that day he was dropped off at school by his parents, never quite ended, despite, a seemingly perpetual longing for it to end. He was far too young to understand what happened then, but nevertheless it left a feeling of emptiness that was difficult for him to understand, much less to come to terms with, at such a tender age. For quite a long time afterwards, there was a feeling of hope deep inside of his very fabric of existence, that harboured an expectation that things would be normal once more, like it used to be before. This provided a sense of comfort that allowed his spirit to survive another day. With time however, that feeling gradually liquified into raw disappointment.

The young Robert gradually withdrew his attention towards interaction with others and became more introverted. At the orphanage, although he was in the company of a lot more people than when he lived his parents, they failed to substitute for the love he had come to know and expect from the people around him. He never grew used to the many different faces that greeted him each day. Some expressed love and care, others did not, but by far, most were indifferent and cold in their interactions with him.

Robert had to adapt quickly to a rigid daily routine, without any room for disobedience or tardiness. The busy days were filled by the endless mechanical modality of existence that lacked the type of unconditional love from a parent which every child deserved. Although resources were limited and thinly distributed amongst the kids of the orphanage, it was that deficient emotional ingredient that Robert sadly missed the most of all.

A bell sounded sharply at six a.m. every day. He was expected to get up and off the bed immediately. He shared a common bedroom with eleven other boys of varying ages. The older boys slept in the higher bunks, almost as a reward for their seniority. But to some, this was more, a medal of courage for surviving whilst being there longer.

Although, there were some school activities during the course of the day, there was a high degree of variability depending on the availability of staff. Robert developed an interest in books early on and went hunting for these in every room that he was allowed to visit. His interest in books only intensified with time and he was noted to be withdrawn a lot of the time. However, unlike many of the others, he was contented reading books than seeking personal interactions or attention.

Tara was a young lady who had just finished high school when she joined the staff at the orphanage. She was hoping to obtain a bit of work-experience before venturing out into the world to conquer a dream that she was yet to conjure up in her mind. She was not tied to ambition or ruled by regimented protocols. Tara was easy-going, caring and compassionate. She was very 'down-to-earth' in her approach to life and this resonated well to the young child, especially, Robert.

To the developing child, Tara was not only less robotic in her approach, but seemed genuinely warm and comforting to him. Finally, there was a place in his world where could gravitate towards in times of emotional need. She was the only one in the institution who had access into Robert's complex emotional world, even in times of his deep emotional self-isolation.

Fortunately for Robert, Tara's temporary stint at the orphanage grew roots into a more substantive post. She progressively worked her way up over the next few years to become the lead educational officer at the institution. By this time, the young Robert had attained an admirably high proficiency in literature and was undoubtedly the most academically-inclined student there. Every morning he would get ready, before everyone else, and fetch the newspaper. He studied the financial section as it were his most prized text book. For his tenth birthday, Tara got him a special present, a book on introductory economics and business management.

A few months later, Robert was summoned to a room where he found the manager and Tara there waiting in there for him. The atmosphere felt tense and serious. He could not work out why he was asked to be there though; whatever it was, it probably was not going to be good. He knew though the suspense was going to short-lived, as he was soon going to find out.

Mrs Helger, the manager, welcomed him and asked him to sit down on a chair on the opposite side of her desk, where Tara was also seated.

'A matter has come up and I would like to discuss it with you,' she started.

"Whenever, a conversation began in that way, there was a tendency that it would lead to something unpleasant," he began thinking to himself. As he turned towards Tara, whom he had come to trust, he noticed a warm feeling of excitement in her eyes.

'We have a lovely couple who have been in touch with us, and they would like to have you live with them,' Mrs Helger continued.

Time paused for moment as the uncertainty and excitement, that a potential massive life-changing event evoked, took over. Robert looked at Tara, her face was all flushed, as she brought her hands to her cheeks with tears in her eyes and a sense of hope and satisfaction in her expression. Robert did not quite know how to interpret this and more so, how to respond. He therefore, opted not to.

'Robert, this is a wonderful opportunity for you to be part of a real family. They seem like a really lovely couple. You would have far more opportunities than you would have here.

And you would have parents who would love and care for you dearly,' said Mrs Helger. 'How do you feel about this, Robert?'

Robert responded, 'Why do I have to leave? All I know is this place and everyone I know is here.'

Tara then interjected, in a soft and warm voice, with tears welling up in her eyes, 'Robert, we love having you here. But this is not even half of a proper life for a young boy like you. You have a whole life ahead of you, a world to explore, a chance to be part of a family again.'

'I already have a life here and you all are my family, why do I need another,' Robert responded sharply.

'Listen, son,' said Mrs Helger, 'I know this is not an easy decision for you and one that would be daunting for you, but you will be much happier living in a normal family, being brought up by loving parents who could provide you with much more opportunities than we would ever be able to here at this home.'

Robert began crying, 'What if it all happens again and I lose my parents... again! What happens then? I don't want to go through this again, please, please...'

Tara rushed over and hugged him tightly and attempted to comfort the frightened young boy.

'Don't worry, my dear, I am sure that they will take really good care of you. You will have your own house; your own room, they will take you out shopping, on trips; it would be wonderful. We will all miss you. But more importantly, we would be happy for you.'

The young Robert eventually settled down gradually warming up to the idea. Mrs Helger informed him that the arrangements were all being finalised and that his new parents would be coming over to take him to his new home — in California.

'Why so far away?' Robert asked.

'It's not that far away,' said Tara reassuringly. 'Sometimes change is a positive thing. Don't be scared.'

It was an emotional week for Robert. He prepared as best as he knew how to. By the end of the week, the world he had come to know, built, interacted with, trusted and depended on was going to dissolve and a new life for him was to be forged. He knew, only too well, that this meant new experiences and new challenges. He did not like change and was reluctant to embrace it. He said his goodbyes and braced for the impending moment of change, and all it was to bring.

Jim and Nancy Serracruz were active socialites who managed to foster a wide circle of friends from various levels of society. They were not blessed with any kids of their own, unfortunately, but had been thinking of the possibility of adopting a child to do their bit to society. They had discussed this with many members of their various social circles who supported this idea and praised their efforts when they eventually took the leap.

Mr and Mrs Serracruz were most delighted to meet their new son. They were quite friendly and warm towards the young boy, who appeared quite shy. Robert had developed quite a quiet and introverted personality over the years at the orphanage. It took him several days to begin to interact with his new parents, even at a basic level.

Over the next few months, the relationship between Robert and his parents began thawing and it eventually blossomed, as the young boy's insecurities of rejection faded. They began engaging in various social activities together. The excitement that his new parents had was so strong, there were no signs of it weaning anytime soon.

Robert was enrolled into one of the best private schools in the state through the help of one of Jim's high-profile contacts. Despite the best efforts of his parents, Robert, unfortunately, found it difficult to settle down there. Everyone, including his peers at school, knew about his personal circumstances, for which he was publicly jeered at. This exacerbated his introverted tendencies to the point where he hardly muttered a word at school and found it extremely difficult to interact with anyone.

It was not long after that his parents were summoned to the school for a meeting. They were told that Robert had special needs, that this school was not the most appropriate for him. They suggested a few other schools that may have the necessary infrastructure and programs in place to help Robert with his problems. This came as a point-blank range bullet, penetrating into the heart of his new parents. He was then transferred out immediately and was then enrolled into another private school, again one which was usually reserved for kids of more privileged background in Californian society.

As time wore on, the young Robert became even more introverted. It was becoming difficult for his parents to encourage him to even participate in conversations at the dinner table. Even worse, his interest in books and reading had evaporated. He was rapidly descending into the darkness of an emotional abyss. They were somewhat concerned and bewildered about his attitude and behaviour. They contacted the previous institution in New York where Robert spent several years previously. They spoke to Tara, the person who knew Robert the best, as she had spent the most time with him.

Tara was most troubled and concerned to hear about his current condition, but made no hesitation in pointing out that this was not the Robert she knew. Something, she thought, was not right and maybe Robert was struggling to cope in his new environment. But why?

'Maybe this needs to probed into a bit more by the appropriately qualified professional at his school,' she suggested.

'Nonsense, he has everything he needs, we have provided him with everything, the best schools the... the best of everything he could have... any kid could have wished for,' retorted Jim.

'Something is obviously, fundamentally wrong with this kid!' he continued.

Tara was most disheartened and upset at his tone of voice and the words he used. She, again, suggested to Jim that Robert maybe experiencing difficulty with adjusting to his new environment or school and he should, maybe, get some help.

Robert's condition was worsening and Jim and Nancy were becoming more and more frustrated daily. Now in the fourth school over the course of eighteen months, Jim received a phone call from the principal one evening, inviting Nancy and him for a meeting about Robert.

At the meeting, they met the principal in his office, along with the school nurse and the lead psychologist for the school.

'Mr and Mrs Serracruz, we understand that Robert has been quite withdrawn. He is having considerable difficulty in settling in,' said the principal in a contemplative manner, while removing his spectacles.

'Well, this is very frustrating for us, as you would imagine. He obviously has a history of mental issues which were not previously declared to us when we adopted him,' said Nancy.

'Well, Mrs Serracruz, not from what we have discovered,' replied the principal, whilst leaning forward over his desk. 'I will now pass you on Mrs Wiley, our lead psychologist, who will explain,' said the tall grey-haired man behind the massive oak desk.

'Mr and Mrs Serracruz, thank you for taking the time to come over today', she began, 'we have picked up on your child's problems early on and have carried out a full clinical investigation. Robert has no detected underlying mental problems. It is not unusual that kids can go into a state of withdrawal when they are under peer pressure, stress or being bullied at school.'

The principal then looked up and took over the conversation.

'We are committed to doing the best we can for your son. We will work with him and yourselves to make him feel safe and secure again. You will be most surprised by the change that you both would notice in the coming weeks to months.'

'How could you be so sure that this is the problem?' asked Jim harshly.

'We are very confident about this' replied Mrs Wiley firmly.

Robert's parents did not seem quite convinced and left without confirming support for the school's plan of intervention. When they got home, both parents had a private conversation between themselves. They felt that Robert's problem was far deeper than that which was made out by the school and, either way, they did not feel that they should allow this to affect their busy lives. They were worried that his needs were complex and this would have a disastrous effect on their lives, their career and their social standing in the local society.

'How will it look if people realise that this kid has some sort of serious mental problem? What will it do for our reputation in the society? We don't have the time in our busy schedules to take him back and forth from one appointment to another,' they agreed.

The next day, they dropped Robert off at school and both parents met at Nancy's office behind closed doors. They talked about it again between themselves, considering things from the context of their lives and their perspectives. Not long after, they arrived at a conclusion that they thought was best for themselves.

They contacted the social welfare department and outlined their desire to end the adoption. This was obviously extremely disappointing for the local agent. There was not much she could have done, really. She considered that Robert may wish to go back to the orphanage in New York, as he was probably struggling to cope on the West Coast. She placed a call over to the institution in New York, transmitting a ray of disappointment to the other side of the country.

When Jim and Nancy told Rob the news, that he was going to be re-homed, surprisingly, they noticed that he was rather indifferent to it. Again, that reaffirmed their opinion that things were not at all right with the boy. But for Rob, he was already at an emotional low point. Any lower, was not even fathomable. At this dark moment in time in his life, when hope seemed invisible through the dark veils of reality, Rob managed to muster the courage to cling on to life. He had been there before, and as much as he disliked it, survival was what was at stake. He knew that he had to concentrate all of his energy on this one goal. Things could only get better.

Tara, the educational lead at his previous orphanage in New York came to find out about the tragic news through her colleague taking the call from California a bit earlier.

'What a lovely boy Robert is!' she exclaimed. 'How much that poor boy must have struggled across there over the last few months.'

She thought that it was just not right for Rob's adoptive parents to give up on him and give him back because he did not fit into their lifestyle any more. Surely a child cannot be managed like a dress that they no longer liked and simply returning it to the store, in the pretext of it having a stain.

Tara, on her own volition, took decisive action. She immediately placed a call to the local social welfare department in California. The conversation that transpired dramatically changed the course of Rob's life, for yet another time.

Chapter 4
Dances with Hope

*True love is as resilient as the soul — it can survive any
storm*

Despite our efforts at times, not everything in life could be
accurately mapped out and meticulously executed, even when
the stakes are the highest, they could possibly be. For if it was,
then we would be a slave to life, at many levels and in many
ways, much like Jim and Nancy. Sometimes, some of the best
and deep-rooted decisions that are taken, are done in haste. To
truly live is to take the bull by the horns when the going gets
tough. Usually at these times there is a lot at stake, but with
firm resolve, with the knowledge that you are doing the right
thing for yourself and others and with unparalleled
commitment, a path for accomplishment may be created. For
these are the ideal ingredients for success.

After learning about the recent experience of the young
Robert and his immediate fate, Tara did something that most
would be afraid to. Something that would have likely scared
the hell out of her, had it been another instance in time, under
different circumstances. Soon afterwards, Tara flew to
California, sought and won the adoption rights of Rob. She
then settled with the kid there on the West Coast. It was the
most daring thing she had done in her entire life. It was one of

the most daring things anyone could have done in their life. She was determined to start all over again from scratch. Only this time, she was blessed with the opportunity to care for a bright and loving kid.

Tara had no problems settling in on the opposite side of the country, and even if she did, this was not the time to harbour negative thoughts or regret. At the height of uncertainty in her life, she decisively pressed on with life, creating cheerfulness every day and loving every moment life offered. She raised Rob as a single parent, working as a teacher at a local high school. This soon developed into a bright chapter in both of their lives.

It was not long before her homesickness faded and she did not miss her old life on the East Coast any more. She quickly became used to the warm dry weather and often wondered why she had not thought about living in California before. She certainly did not miss the rather harsh and gloomy winters that she faced in New York. But of course, New York was all she knew. She was brought up there and enjoyed the comforts and benefits of being part of a large family.

For most of her adult years in New York, however, she found herself busy trying to carve out a life from solid rocks. Her family later dispersed and for a while she was all alone. Everything felt like a perpetual uphill struggle to her. Her attempts at several relationships failed for one reason or another. But this did not discourage her, as she kept trying, and this was all she knew; until now. Sometimes miracles, disguised as change, are born from the bowels of despair.

For the first time in her adult life, Tara felt happy and contented. Life now had a purpose. Something to look forward to everyday. Had she not worked at the orphanage for some six years or so, the pieces that would have eventually made her life whole would not have been uncovered or brought her life perfectly together like this. The journey of life takes mysterious turns here and there; some for the worse but eventually with patience and hope, the pieces usually fall together.

Tara spent a lot time together with Rob. Life began unfolding beautifully for this little family, in ways that neither of them could have imagined. Time flew by effortlessly. She often took the young Rob to bookshops, his favourite place in the whole world. He could spend hours in there, browsing through books of all genres, but was especially interested in those related to business and finance.

All the issues Rob had developed when he first came to California resolved once he started at a new public high school. He fitted in better with the other kids, made friends almost seamlessly and engaged with others a whole lot more. His academic performance improved significantly and he was soon recognised as the 'whiz kid' in his class.

Rob graduated from high school as the valedictorian of his class and won a scholarship to study law at the prestigious, Stanford University. Tara could not have been any prouder of him, and reiterated her mantra to the young man regarding the direct relationship between hard work and success. She taught him to always aim high to realise his full capabilities. She knew that he was full of potential and was an extremely bright person. The sky was the limit for him.

Throughout the rest of his high school years, the two became closer and closer, as their emotional ties strengthened. They were inseparable. At that instance in time, neither could have hoped for a more fulfilling life. Rob always made time for his adopted mom and Tara was completely devoted to him.

Robert coped reasonably well during his first year in law school. Although this was not the field that Rob was most passionate about, he worked hard at it because he knew it would make Tara happy. She constantly dreamt of him being a successful lawyer and living a better than comfortable life with a family of his own.

Towards the end of Rob's first year at university, tragedy struck. Tara was diagnosed with breast cancer. Although she tried her best to keep this tragic bit of news from Rob, she could not do so for very long. They were so close to each other that it was difficult for either of them to keep secrets from each other. One day, she decided, that it was not the right thing to keep something, so significant as this was, from him, primarily because she needed put things into place for the future. She wanted to reassure herself that Rob would have a settled life going forwards, should things not work out the way that the doctors were hoping they would.

Hearing about this news from his mom felt like being pierced with an arrow through his chest, shattering his heart into bits. He knew though that, he not only had to be strong, but he had to project this strength, in her presence, to help her to alleviate her worries.

"How painful this must have been for her?" he thought. He bent over and hugged her tightly, promising that they will both get over this together. He also promised to be at her side every step of the way in her fight of this malady.

Over the next year, Tara went through the wars with her illness. Rob tried his best to accompany her to the medical appointments, as many times as he could. Soon afterwards, she was advised by her doctor to prepare to have radical surgery in order to treat the tumour as it had progressed.

'Is this surgery going to completely eradicate the disease?' Rob asked the doctor.

'Yes and no,' the tired-looking doctor replied with a stern look that was devoid of any facial expression. 'We will attempt to remove all of the tumour. But even if we were successful, we cannot cure the condition.'

'How likely is it to recur then?' the young man asked, concerned.

The doctor leaned over to Rob and with a steady low-pitched voice, said to him in a caring way, 'Son, unfortunately, although we have made significant advances with this type of cancer in the last five years, we still do not have any significant effective treatments. The prognosis is not all that great I'm afraid, but surgery should help to slow the progress of the disease.'

It wasn't a great moment for either Tara or Rob. But if life had taught him anything, it was that despite it all, the only constant in life was the need to embrace the challenges it posed and to fight them as hard as possible. This mantra was reflected in Tara's titanic strength and courage throughout her life. The greatest lessons in life are learnt, not from books or lectures, but from the code laid down through manner real titans face life.

All throughout this ordeal, Rob missed many classes and tutorials at university. He was beginning to find it difficult to catch-up. This was reflected in his poor grades throughout the year. But it did not deter his resolve to do all he can to support the light of his existence, even though he felt completely helpless at changing the inevitable outcome. Her predetermined fate was becoming more and more obvious.

Tara's surgery went well but she experienced multiple complications during her recovery and spent several distressing days in hospital. Once her wounds had healed and everything appeared to be going in the right direction, she was told that she needed to undergo a course of radiotherapy over several weeks.

She bravely embraced this. Rob never left her side. Following the radiotherapy, she needed to have chemotherapy as the tumour had spread to her lungs. Although she felt well, her doctor advised her to consider the additional treatment, as there was little else he could offer her.

The chemotherapy was extremely unpleasant, and not unexpectedly so. She went through a period of hell whilst on the toxins. She felt the poison destroying, not only the cancer, but herself from inside out — cell by cell. At the end, she felt numb emotionally, as she could not physically recognise herself in the mirror any more. But nevertheless, she remained strong and persistent, surviving mostly on the love she had for her son and his for her.

Watching her deteriorate like this was emotionally distressing for Robert. But the young man did not have any real reasonable choices. He had to follow the script of life that was somehow pre-written for him. He did not have any other family and no suitably close friends to help or support him. He did not have the luxury of a safety net, in some form or the other, as most do. That buffer between himself and the vagaries of life was painfully and noticeably absent.

Tara made it through chemo missing bits of herself. Some were easily replaceable; others were not so. She wore a wig when going out but never quite felt like herself again. The ordeal she had been through over the last year or so was starting to drain her emotionally, as well as psychologically. She thought to herself that maybe she ought to start making some plans for her future, since she may not bear witness to it for very much longer.

Tara wanted to provide Robert with something that he could find comfort in during the difficult times life would throw at him in the future, something that would encourage him to be strong and determined, something that make him happy for the rest of his life… something that would love him, support him like she did… something that could replace her when she was no longer.

She spent quite a while to herself brainstorming what this should be. The perfect answer was not an easy ask here, though. How does a mom replace herself when she is gone, and also equally, how can one find a replacement for a mom? It is impossible. Finally, she thought that the best solution was probably, not something physical at all, but maybe something as simple and humble as a string of caring words. This would definitely survive eternity.

She started drafting a letter to the young man, to let him know how much she cared for him, what he meant to her and how much he has changed her life. Innumerable thoughts raced through her busy mind. Too much to condense into a letter but too little to see a loved one through the rest of his life. She decided to sleep on it for a bit as she had become very exhausted by then.

Her condition deteriorated rapidly soon afterwards. She was taken to hospital. A body scan revealed that the tumour had extensively metastasised within her body. Robert had a private word with the doctor outside her room.

'Doctor, is my mom going to make it?' the worried young man asked.

'Can I be honest with you?' he started. 'Things do not look good at this stage. We could consider another cycle of chemotherapy, but even so, the chances of survival are pretty slim.'

'Would chemo make her live longer?' he asked, with a shaky voice and with tears building up in his eyes.

'Marginally, weeks maybe,' the doctor replied, 'but the side-effects can be quite uncomfortable.'

'And without chemo?' Rob asked, struggling to hold the tears back.

'Days,' said the doctor, pausing for a moment in deep contemplation. 'Yes, we are talking, days really,' he said, nodding his head in agreement with his own answer.

It was a difficult situation and an even more difficult decision to make. Every minute more he could spend with his mom would be like an eternity to him. He would do anything to have an extra moment with her. But at the same time, he could not bear the thought of having to witness her suffer in the manner she did when she had chemo before. He wiped his tears away, straightened his spine and returned to her room, projecting an image of strength.

Tara was rapidly becoming weaker and weaker. She resisted the idea of having another cycle of chemo and did not feel strong enough to discuss this with Rob. Rob sat by her side throughout the day. Tara reminded him of his end-of-year exams which were scheduled for the next day. Rob tried to have it rescheduled but she insisted that he should go and take the exams. She had every faith in him. Far more than he did in himself, at that point in time.

Rob promised to returned to the hospital straight after the exams to be with her the following day. Her condition continued to deteriorate dramatically over the course of the next morning. She asked the nurse, attending to her, for a sheet of paper and a pen. Although she did not have much of a chance to prepare that special parting present she wanted for Rob, at that instant, she now knew the best present she could leave him.

She was so weak she was unable to sit up in bed. She managed to roll herself to the left with the aid of her weight and gravity, barely held on to the pen between her fingers. She wrote him a brief but powerful message. A message that would guide him through all of the dances with fate that he was yet to experience in his still young life.

Not long after she scribbled the message down on a loose sheet of paper, she left this world, leaving behind a priceless gift of words to her beloved son.

Chapter 5
Dances with Threats and Opportunities

Life's too short to not be bold!

An unwelcomingly loud, repetitively screeching sound jolted Rob's attention from a dream that was hurriedly erased from his memory the minute his consciousness returned. He was then awake. He managed to catch a glimpse at the clock, near the bedside, with the large green digits. Four o'clock it was flashing repeatedly. This was his wake-up call, that morning, as it was every morning since he started his job over two years ago. After waking, he read for two hours before getting ready to go to work. It was the best part of the day for him, for reading helped him to maintain his sanity.

It was now two years since Tara passed on. Robert was finding it difficult to cope and he had even dropped out of law school. The emotional burden of her illness and losing her were far too much for him. He was trying his utmost to overcome this though, and was on the road to emotional recovery.

He started off as an office assistant at a local newspaper company and was only promoted to the post of PA for a journalist three months before. He had an old, but reliable, car that took him back and forth from work, the whole 100-mile journey every day. Sadly, it was the closest thing he had to a friend. They shared a tiny universe together. The highlight of his journey every day was the dances he had with the sunrise and sunset on the horizon while meandering along the curves of the freeway, to and from work. There was not much else to look forward to in his life, otherwise.

One morning, he came across an advertisement in the newspaper. Someone had a revolutionary idea of creating a product that could potentially store large amounts of data using a computer. The inventor was looking for an investor to take his idea forward. This piqued Robert's interest, although he did not know a whole lot about computers except that, they were massive devices, probably large enough to fill the inside of a building, and were capable of performing magical tasks.

After work that evening, he phoned the number on the newspaper advert, and spoke to a gentleman whose speech was so fast in pace that his words almost landed one on top of the other. But it was still decipherable though, with some attention. This guy, called Alan, managed to convince Rob about the great potential of his idea. He needed an investment of $50,000 to convert his idea into reality. This was going to be problem for the young office assistant-cum-PA, if he intended to invest into Alan's idea. But he hated his job so much and, at the same time, had a roaring passion for business. He was desperate to not let this opportunity pass him by.

That night was a sleepless one for Rob, as his mind could not find a resting place to settle down. He brainstormed every possible way to raise the funds. By the morning, he had concocted a plan. He later phoned Alan and arranged a meeting in person over a cup of coffee the day after. Whilst back at work that day, he asked his boss for some time off the following morning, however, it was going to be a busy day at the office, so his request was declined.

Rob was quite disappointed about this as he found himself in a dilemma. He decided to accept his boss's decision and had planned to cancel his appointment with Alan when he got home that evening. His boss was unhappy with Rob's request, after all he was just a PA, he thought. His boss acted quite petulantly towards Rob for the rest of the day. He asked him to make numerous cups of coffee, even when he was not even drinking them, and ordered him to work throughout his lunch break, without as much as a minute's rest.

Rob did not like this job, but did it because he needed an income, but more importantly, he needed it as therapy to overcome his grief. As his boss stepped out for his fifth break of the day, Rob decided to check that he had enough money to pay for the petrol for his car when he left that day. He opened his wallet carefully and a folded piece of paper dropped off. It was a piece of paper that meant a lot to him. It was the paper that his mom had left for him the day she passed on. It was her last gift to him. He had never before had the courage to read what was scribbled on that sheet, as he thought doing so would lead to closure of his lost. Although he was not quite prepared to do so before then, maybe the time had finally come to do so, he thought to himself.

He picked up the paper from the floor, placed his wallet on the desk and proceeded to carefully unfold it. When he read it, his eyes flooded with grief that changed, almost instantly, to gratification. The message was one sentence long. It read:

"My dear Rob, promise me that you would do one thing for me; follow your heart always, no matter what comes your way. Love you dearly always, Mom."

He had just managed to wipe his tears away when his boss walked in.

'What the hell are doing?' he shouted at him. 'Shouldn't you be working rather than using company's time as your personal time?'

Robert looked up him, gave him a stare that his boss would never forget for the rest of his life, even if he did manage to forget what he told him next.

'Sir, I have done the best I could for you and this company. I believe that I have fulfilled my ambitions here. I therefore quit, as of now.'

'"Your ambitions"? What gives you the right to think that you are worthy of having "ambitions"? You are just a glorified post-boy!' shouted the angry man at him.

Robert chose not to answer and walked directly towards the door as the man looked on. As he walked through the doors, he experienced a relaxing feeling, as if the weight of a mountain was lifted off his shoulders. He walked away happy, because at that moment, for the first time in his life, he was able to act exactly as he felt and take the reins of life in his own hands. He could feel it in the depths of his bones that something immensely exciting was on the horizon.

The following day, for the very first time, he welcomed the sound of the alarm at four a.m. He carried on with his reading as usual and prepared his plans afterwards for his meeting with Alan later that day. It was a gorgeously sunny day, so Rob decided to wait outside the coffee shop to greet Alan. Then he could enjoy the fresh air of peace for a few moments. From a distance, he saw a slightly chubby, round-faced gentleman, wearing a brown bowling shirt with flower-patterned stripes, invitingly approaching.

'You must be Robert Lancaster,' said the man.

'I am,' Rob responded and offered his hand out. The gesture was immediately reciprocated by Alan.

'Nice to meet you,' said Robert, 'shall we go inside, then?'

Robert and Alan hit it off at once. Their personalities merged with each other's with little effort or expenditure. This was made somewhat easier as their interests dovetailed each other's well. Robert found out that Alan, who was an engineer, with a major interest in physics and computing, had an idea that could prove to be revolutionary.

Alan found a way to compress and store information into a tiny plastic disc. Robert could not understand how this was even at all possible, but neither could he have imagined how this was possible with cassette tapes at the time.

'Information is not only power, but it is the future,' Alan told him.

'Have you had any interest from any other investor?'

'Yes, I have had some but they will not willing to give it the priority it deserves. Look, believe me, this is the future!' pleaded Alan.

Robert was soon sold on the idea after this brief chat with Alan. But the difficult aspects of the conversation set in — the financial bits. Alan became a bit sceptical that Rob did not have the funds necessary.

'How can you afford to invest in my idea if you are a PA?' asked Alan. 'And don't take this the wrong way, but you are quite young.'

'I have some assets which I am going to sell to raise the money,' he responded, 'please just leave it up to me to come up with the money.'

'How much time do you need then?' asked the blonde engineer.

'Six months,' replied Rob.

'Rob, you seem like a nice guy and all, but I am sitting on dynamite here. I can't afford to wait so long. All I could give you is two weeks,' said Alan firmly but in a friendly tone of voice, as by then he had developed a liking for the young entrepreneur. He wondered what it would be like to work with this fine young man, rather than with someone else who he may not get on with.

Rob replied equally firmly, 'It's a deal then!'

They shook hands and agreed to meet up again after two weeks. In the meantime, Rob had managed to convince his counterpart to terminate his search for further investors.

Rob left facing a challenging dilemma. He had to raise a relatively large sum of funds in under two weeks. He had thought carefully about this, and fulfilling to his promise to his mom, he decided to be bold about it. He made the decision to sell the property that Tara had left him to cover the expenses. This was all he had to his name financially, but deep down inside, he believed that this was a gamble worth taking, despite the obvious high risks involved. There was something about Alan that impressed Rob and he therefore, decided to put all his trust in him.

Rob managed to raise the raise the funds in one week because he proceeded to sell the property for a reduced price, just enough to cover the capital required for the investment only. Robert was now working on a tight budget and managed to plan well in order to survive for the next four to six months. He had to do so with a daily budget of less than two dollars. But this was the least of the challenges that bothered him at the time. He sealed the deal with Alan two weeks later, and together, they founded their company, Shudard and Lancaster Digital Enterprises Limited.

To cover his modest living expenses in the meantime, he tried to sell his car. This proved to be the most difficult of all however, as the old Chevrolet had long past seen its glory days and, for all intents and purposes, it had already outlived its expiry date. So, as it proved impossible to get the car sold, he was unable to raise the funds to stay at the local hostel. Therefore, he had no choice but to sleep in the vehicle at nights.

However, after three months, he did manage to get a decent amount though for the car, from a company on the outskirts of the town, who purchased it for 150 dollars. Their interest in it was for its parts, but mostly for harvesting its metal. He found it a bit difficult to part with the car. But life is full of hard decisions and this was not the time to get too sentimental or emotional about it. He was then able to afford to stay at a local hostel for a rate of a dollar a night.

During that time, both Rob and Alan worked practically around the clock trying a develop a prototype for their product. They were hoping that it would revolutionise the way data were stored, not only for large scale applications, but also for the regular users of the new age of computer technology. They frequently encountered obstacles of varying severity that required their utmost resolve to overcome at times. They were both concretely determined. They had to be, as both of their lives depended on it so much, more so than could be emphasised.

Finally, after four months, their product — a type of plastic disc that was able to store more information than any other regular device at the time — was ready to be tested. They pitched it to the largest computer manufacturer in California at the time. Much to Rob's and Alan's delight, the company was extremely amazed about it. They offered to take on production and marketing of the disc and offered the duo a decent weekly stipend until the final product was ready for marketing on a large-scale basis.

After receiving his first pay check, he finally could have afforded a decent meal (which he had not had in months), and to treat himself even more, he decided to attended a concert at the Hollywood Bowl. Little did he know that this decision would add colour and dimension to life in ways impossible to imagine. His life changed forever. It was at that concert, on that night, that he met his lovely Margot.

The contractual agreement with the computer company went on for a year while the product was being manufactured and tested. During this time, Rob managed on his stipend. He worked long hours, but at the same time enjoyed dating the lovely young musician he had met at the concert hall. One evening, after one of her concerts, Robert took Margot for an amorous wander through the dimly lit streets, which were ripe with romance and adventure. As they meandered their way along the pavement of the pavilion, he stopped before of a string quartet playing a new hit at the time, *The Roses of Picardy,* the music of which infused the air with love.

At the end of the musical performance, whilst the other couples in attendance started applauding, Rob went down on his knees before the love of his life.

'Margot, my love. You have become a part of me that I can't live without any more. I do not want to be incomplete any more. Would you please marry me?' he asked.

Before he could finish, she replied, 'Yes, oh yes, I love you so much. Yes, I would... yes, I would!'

The small crowd applauded thunderously at the newly engaged. The quartet was then inspired by what they had just witnessed and participated in their celebration by offering their finest performance. The night sky lit up with excitement as the universe opened up its heart, pouring its love and blessings onto the young couple.

Chapter 6
Dances with Family

Success is ignited with a strong sense of passion

It was a beautiful evening, bathed with innumerable golden rays of sunshine as the sun offered its final hurrah before settling down that evening. It was indeed a desired pleasure to be in its warmth, staring at the sparkles dancing on the surface of the water as they greeted the millions of ripples.

Robert, dressed in a dark blue pin-striped Italian suit, stood outside the doors of one of the best restaurants, in all of California, clutching on to a large bouquet of the most beautiful flowers imaginable. Margot was running a few minutes late. As she arrived, he presented her with his lovely smile and a warm kiss on her cheek. The bouquet was almost as beautiful as the recipient.

Robert had invited Margot to celebrate their wedding anniversary that evening. For weeks, he had been racking his brain to come up with the best anniversary present for her. He knew that she deserved only the best. The restaurant boasted three Michelin stars and was anchored cosily along the edge of the coastal waters. The ambience inside was incredible and unrivalled.

'How time flies when you are having fun,' whispered Margot.

'Yes, my love, I could hardly believe that it has been three years. Undoubtedly, the three most enjoyable years of my life.'

'Yes, for me too,' she added and reached out her arm to stroke his cheek lovingly.

'I did not believe it was possible, but I find myself loving you more and more each day! How is that even possible?' she asked, as she flashed a lovingly mischievous grin at her husband.

They began reminiscing about their time together. The couple was married in a small private ceremony shared only with Rob's business partner, and now best friend, and an entire orchestra of musicians, who were all colleagues of the talented bride. Noticeably absent, were relatives — close and far. Although Rob did not have any known relatives, Margot chose not invite any of hers, not even her parents.

Margot was still mad about the way her parents treated the love of her life. She had not communicated with them since that fateful day when she had taken Rob to meet them. Her parents were quite harsh about her relationship to Rob and ordered for it to end immediately. Although, time is a force capable of diluting pain and disappointment, her anger and obstinacy towards her parents never quite faded. Maybe not enough time had passed.

Shortly after their engagement, Rob was given an incredible surprise from the computer company he had put a lot of resources and effort into. Finally, the hard work and determination was about to pay off. The results were encouraging and the international team of scientists and engineers had found a way to mass-produce the product. A letter came through both of their mailboxes, officially requesting that Rob and Alan met with the company's CEO and board of directors.

Rob donned his usual casual t-shirt and jeans and waited for Alan to pick him up. Alan, on the hand, had an intuitive whiff that this was not going another ordinary meeting. Therefore, he added a brown tweed jacket to his outfit in preparation. As they arrived, there were a couple of black-suited men waiting in the lobby to greet them. They then took them up to the boardroom.

They were asked to take a seat on the most comfortable cushions that Robert had ever sat on, while one of the gentlemen went off to announce their arrival to the CEO. He returned and ask the two entrepreneurs to follow him. As the door opened, they both felt intimidated as they found a room-full of immaculately-dressed men and women sitting around, possibly, the largest 'dining table' that Rob had ever seen. All eyes were on them that morning. They were the sole focus of everyone's attention.

The neatly combed, grey-haired, medium built gentleman at the head of the 'dinner table' rose up from his seat to greet them.

'Gentlemen, welcome!' he said with a loud booming voice. 'Please have a seat, both of you,' he continued, as he used his hand to motion them to sit on the two empty seats at the opposite end of the table.

'Thank you for accepting my invitation and for coming over today.'

'We have been excited about your idea ever since the inception. My team has worked hard at evaluating its global applications and usefulness. You are not only great entrepreneurs, but you are visionaries! You are able to see the future of the world in ways that most of us can't. I applaud you both!'

Both Rob and Alan felt a bit at ease now that they have been praised by the eldest man around the large table. But, neither Rob nor Alan were at all sure what to say or how to respond to this. For one thing, the ambience of the room severely intimated them, as it was like none other either of the two men had experienced before.

Fortunately, the CEO continued speaking.

'I have discussed this at length with the board members present here today and we have arrived at the unanimous conclusion to offer you a deal; we would like to buy your idea, or should we say, intellectual property.'

He stopped to gauge the facial expression of the two entrepreneurs. The both were unmistakeably excited. The experienced CEO then continued.

'We have considered, in detail, what a fair amount for this would be and would like to offer you one million dollars. How do you both feel about this?' he asked, leaning his tall bodily frame forward across the table with a piercing stare.

At first, both Rob and Alan were completely shocked by the offer. 'A million dollars!! Wow, Wow, wow!' But as the shock lingered inside of Alan, Robert was the first to speak out.

'I am sorry we cannot accept this offer in its current form!' he thundered from the opposite side of the table with a level of confidence that shocked Alan, but more importantly shocked himself, even more. "Where did this confidence suddenly appeared from?"

'This is ground-breaking stuff, it is dynamite, and you know that, you all know it. Please do not insult us with this meagre offer.'

Alan's head rotated ninety degrees to the right and stared right at Rob.

"What the hell is he doing? He is well out of depth here...we are going to lose out on this lucrative deal!" he thought to himself. But he had come to know Rob quite well by now and decided to put his trust in him after all. He knew that Rob was a hundred and ten percent as passionate about this deal as he was.

There was an uncomfortable silence in the room after Rob's last remark. This made, even Rob, feel that maybe he had pushed things a bit too far. One of the board members elected to speak, after clearing his throat first.

'This is the best we can offer. You are free not to accept it, but we would be delighted if you did.'

This was followed by an almost continuous low humming of noise in the room from everyone trying to talk to each other, as quietly as possible, at the same time.

'Ladies and gentlemen, order please!' It was the CEO.

Looking squarely at Rob unblinkingly, he said, 'Mr Lancaster, you have a made an interesting point. I want to reassure you that my board members and myself very much value your talent, idea and product, and as such, we would like you both to know we honour transparency and fairness in all of our transactions.'

Rob was now convinced that he had made a mistake, but before he could try to rectify it, the grey-haired gentleman at the top of table continued speaking.

'Furthermore, I wish to point out to you and your colleague that this is a negotiation and we would welcome your thoughts on the matter. We would be most interested to hear what you consider to be a fair offer and why.'

Rob breathed a sigh of relief but Alan started breathing heavily again.

'We would like a sum of ten million dollars, to have a share of the royalties from the product and to be on the managerial board of this division of your company,' he spelt out to the chairman and the board members.

Again, there was deafening silence in the room.

The chairman, leaned forward on his chair placing both hands onto the table and said,

'Gentlemen, I can offer you one million dollars and ten percent of the royalties and managerial posts for you both within the data product division but... but... I own you... both!'

As he said the last phrase, his voice increased dramatically in tone and emphasis.

'I have no doubts that both of you would use every ounce of your talent to ensure that this venture is successful. I would expect you both to work as hard as you have to ensure this is a success. You can look forward to days merging with nights, all in a blur, and vice versa!' the chairman informed them in an authoritarian tone of voice. 'Is this going to be acceptable to you both?'

Rob looked at Alan and they both nodded in unison before their mutual excitement permitted them to communicate their decision verbally. They had scored the deal of a lifetime, despite the odds being as infinitely small as they were.

This was the start of a brand, new direction in Rob's life that fitted perfectly well with his romantic adventure with his young girlfriend, Margot. A few months later they got married, moved to a new house in the suburbs, and started living the life that Rob and Margot always dreamt of.

They both felt as if they had everything they could have ever wanted, as they reminisced in the romantic ambience of the restaurant, on that special evening marking three years of absolute bliss in their lives.

Unknown to Rob on that special evening, was that Margot had some news she was dying to share with him, but she was waiting for the right moment. After dinner, while they were both sipping on a glass of champagne, she thought the moment was right. She broke the news to him that she was pregnant with their first child. He was delighted! He stood up, walked over to her and hugged her tightly. This was possibly the best news that they could have had.

It was only then, that Rob realised that Margot had not touched her champagne. It all made perfect sense! They wasted no time as they began discussing what the baby would be like, the beautiful clothes they would need to get for her or him and how magical their lives would be. They were both drowning in the intoxication of that magical moment, considering all the mundane aspects associated with parenthood. For now, they were overjoyed about the fact they were going to be parents. And the feeling was surreal.

In the midst of this happy moment, Rob thought that it was a good idea to bring up the issue of Margot's parents. Despite her vowing never to have anything more to do with them, Rob encouraged her to reach out to them. He did not want for her to lose a chance to enjoy the joys of having parents and spending time with them. But more importantly, he did not wish for her to live her life with a lingering feeling of regret once they had passed away.

After Rob brought it up, the mood that evening declined dramatically. It actually upset her and she simply asked to go home. This was not a subject she felt that she wanted to discuss at the time. It was not clear to Robert why she was so stubborn about this. After all, it was her parents' right to like him, or equally, not like him, and whichever it was did not bother him in the slightest. But for Margot it was much more than this. She could not accept that her parents did not trust her well enough to allow her to make her own decision.

They both shared all the wonderful moments and joy that came with the following nine months. It felt like more than a lifetime to Margot, as she could not wait to meet her son. Rob was in a constant state of euphoria at the thought of become a father. There was nothing that could have dampened that feeling.

The birth was uncomplicated and both mom and baby were discharged from the hospital later that evening. Rob drove them both home from the hospital in the middle of the night. Raindrops of blessings pelted down from the heavens above onto the windscreen of the car. Rob felt the need to be extremely cautious and drove at twenty miles per hour for the full length of the journey, taking the baby home for the first time.

Oscar grew up quickly before their eyes. He was extremely clever, but always a reserved child. He preferred books than balls, studying than socialising and writing than riding. Most surprising of all though, he appeared not be interested in music, unlike his parents. This was disappointing, but something both Rob and Margot were happy to accept.

In the early years, Rob was becoming more and more immersed into the business and tried his best to carve out as much time as he could to spend with his son. However, despite his best efforts, Oscar ended up spending most of his time with Margot throughout his early years. It was immensely exhausting for them both, but unspeakably enjoyable.

At the age of four, Oscar was enrolled into one of the most prestigious private schools. He struggled to settle down initially, but this improved with time. Around this time, Robert was becoming quite experienced in business management and was feeling quite confident financially. This confidence incited a desire to take on another bold step, going forward.

Chapter 7
Dances with the Challenges of Life

Everyone is fighting their own war. If we all fought the same war, existence would melt away

It was a gorgeous morning, as Robert arrived at the little café where he met Alan several years ago. That aromatic, unassuming oasis had a kind of a magic of its own. The feeling was inviting, relaxing and embracing. This brought back vivid memories of the one other time he was there. This time he was now a bit older, wiser, more financially secure, but most importantly, unlike the last time, he had now had a family and a friend.

"Why have I not been back here before today?" Robert wondered to himself.

There was a chime as the front door opened, with the creaking sound of rusty hinges, and in walked in, without any doubt, his best friend. He was wearing a black suit and looking sartorially elegant. His hair was still outstandingly blond but with a few more greys in the mix. It was Alan.

They both sat and savoured the heavenly-scented brew without any attempt at being proletarian. The beauty of simplicity was impressive. They exchanged friendly remarks and talked about the success of their business. Robert thought it was the right moment to discuss his plans with his colleague.

'Alan, I have been thinking recently, I do not see myself in this role forever. I would like to pursue my dream as an investor and in business development. Here we are tied to this company,' he stated. 'Please don't get me wrong, they are fantastic, but I would feel unfilled if I don't explore my dreams and passions a bit more.'

'What you are saying, Rob?'

'Listen, Alan, you are my dear friend and I would consider keeping things as they are, if that is what you wish.'

'Rob, but you haven't told me what you want... what do you want?' Alan asked, in a reassuring but assertive tone of voice.

'I do not know if this is the right time, but I am thinking about selling my shares in the company and I would like you to give you the first preference to buy them and so, you could own the company outright.'

Robert continued, 'I am thinking of setting up a company to manufacture a new processor for computers that would be cheap and it would make computers readily available to average householders, not just in California or this country for that matter, but for the whole world.'

'Rob, you are crazy! But you know, it is your strong point, I know.'

'Alan, you are free to join me if you like. We could sell this company and use the funds for this new project. You and me. The A-Team!'

'You know this is risky. Risky to an unfathomably crazy degree!' Alan replied. 'For Christ's sake, we could lose everything!'

'Or we could conquer the world! You don't get anywhere without taking chances, my friend,' said Rob with the passion of a lion.

There was silence for more than a moment at their table, creating a vacuum which was rapidly filled with Rob's hopes that Alan would see the opportunity as clearly as he did. Alan, quietly sat there and sipped on his coffee while Rob looked on. He was not ready to speak as his brain was overloaded with the sheer magnitude of Robert's suggestion. He needed time to compute his response, which needed to be precise, before he could speak again.

'Rob, you are a genius and a great guy. You know that I have always believed in you. But I think this one is too risky, my friend,' said Alan in a sombre tone of voice smacking his lips once or twice as he did so.

'But if you like and if it would help, yes, I would buy your share of the company. But this idea of yours is risky, and as your friend, I have to point that out to you.'

'You are a true friend and gentleman, Al, thank you.'

The gentlemen then stood up, shook hands and went their different ways. Robert was an ambitious, young entrepreneur who thought that he must see and explore everything that he was passionate about. After all, life was far too short not to. There were many cases of similar start-up companies failing and going bankrupt in this line of industry at the time and Alan, being the great friend that he was, rightly warned Rob about the inherent risks. And after all, there was no real need to scream out for change as they were both doing very well professionally and financially. But each individual has their calling in life and sometimes no one else could see or understand why some actions are taken, in one way or the other, or for the reasons that they are taken.

Rob had now gained the experience and financial resources to build his own new company up from scratch. He realised early on, he needed to aim for the stars. He had ambitious goals and once again, he had to put everything on the line to achieve this. Failure was not an option. Not the last time, and certainly not this time.

He designed a robust and pioneering corporate structure to oversee the management of his company, hired the most ambitious and talented people in the field and settled for nothing less than perfection. He saw a need to micromanage all operations until there was palpable and tangible success that he could feel, taste and touch without a hint of doubt. As a result, he was spending more and more hours at work. This worried Margot to the extent that she had to have a discussion with him about it one evening.

'Darling, why are you allowing yourself to get sucked into this so much?' she asked.

Rob was a bit surprised that she would ask this question. To him, she should know just how important it was for the company to succeed and the consequences of failure to do so.

'Darling, I am really sorry, but there is no other way. We just cannot afford to fail!' he exclaimed.

'But it is too much; not good for you, not good for us, not good for our son, who you barely see... just not good!' she screamed.

In an attempt to calm her down, he walked over and hugged her. He tried his best to reassure her. He promised to create more time for both Oscar and her. But although he tried his best, it was a difficult ask... much too difficult; almost impossible. He tried his best to micromanage the operations less and even hired more professionals to take on these roles. However, this company was being built on ambition and Robert's attention was in high demand. There was always something that needed his opinion, his consent and his eye. Pre-empting potential disasters was crucial to its survival, especially in these early times.

Despite his best efforts to spend more time at home with his family, whom he loved with all of his being, unfortunately, he was slowly losing the battle.

"Once we get our prototype done and tested, then I will be a free man again," he thought to himself.

He even came up with a lot of different plans he wanted to do with his wife and son once this was over. During this critical time however, he survived only on the euphoria of these dreams. Margot, on the other hand, was struggling to survive with a young child to look after and an absent husband. She was becoming increasingly weary and frustrated. She started feeling constantly depressed and even struggled with routine day-to-day activities.

Margot was always supportive of the business and Robert. She also yearned for it to be a great success. Despite this, their fights occurred more frequently, fuelled more and more by miscommunication and anger. These became more and more intense. Robert struggled to understand why things had changed. Clearly, they were both viewing things through different lenses. Nevertheless, he tried to support her emotionally, as best as he can.

The company was growing rapidly and finally, they were able to mass produce affordable processors for microcomputers at a price that was economically viable and affordable. They secured a massive contract with a leading computer company that used their processors to build computers. Robert had realised his dream at last.

The family by then had moved to a five-hundred-acre estate in the countryside, where they lived in a mansion with all the luxury amenities that came with it. The house had an impressive foyer with marble tiles and herculean double-spiral staircases leading to the first floor. There were four gigantic outdoors pools and two indoors. The impeccably manicured garden was like a scene from a fairy-tale. It was a ten-minute drive from the entrance gates, along the long curvy drive, to reach the house. It was all impressive on a grand scale.

Happiness is a strange thing. It is almost impossible to understand. In some weird way, it seems to defy the laws of quantum mechanics. The more one tries to seek it out, the more evasive it becomes. But, even stranger, it is not as rare a commodity, as one would expect. It is just that, when it presents itself, it seems to do so effortlessly. The more you search for it, the more it elusive it becomes. Although it would be foolish to try to attempt to tame happiness with the expectation that it would follow the general laws that govern physics, it seems that it is attracted by sheer simplicity. It seems that, as life becomes more complicated, happiness is repelled.

Robert had tried on several occasions to encourage his other half to reach out to her parents so that the elderly couple could meet their grandson, who was growing up into a young man so fast. However, he had learnt to approach this sensitive issue with caution, as it always resulted in Margot becoming upset. Robert suspected that this was a significant cause for Margot's unhappiness which was now overflowing into their lives, and it had even started manifesting in her interactions with Oscar. It was however, difficult to discuss it with her. And especially in their grand house, there was more space for Margot to hide from her emotional problems. Loneliness only served to fuel her unhappiness.

The couple made the decision to send Oscar to boarding school at the age of eleven. They both thought this was the best school for him and the best education they could provide him with. Robert communicated with him every night and Oscar grew to appreciate this. His bond with his mom, however, was stronger. She missed him a lot and this inevitably also contributed to her unhappiness as it fuelled her loneliness even more.

Margot became more and more emotionally distanced from her husband. Rob felt helpless and increasingly frustrated. He thought that did everything he could to try to reach out to her emotionally, but that door was now closing in on him. This became increasingly worrying for him.

A few years later, during dinner at home, he decided that he could not stand this any more.

'Honey, I think we need to speak… we need to talk about the elephant in the room.'

After a significant delay, she looked up and stared him in the eyes for the first time, for as long as he could remember.

'What do want to talk about?' she enquired coldly.

'You know that I love you dearly, you mean to world to me,' he began. 'I don't like it that we seem to fight about petty, silly things so much. What is wrong with us?'

'Is something wrong with us?' she asked in a low monotonous voice.

'Do we need to be like this all the time?' he asked.

'What is wrong to you?' she screamed at him.

Robert realised that he was not getting very far with the conversation but still decided to bring up the issue of her parents.

'Does it worry you that you haven't been in touch with your parents for such a long time? I don't want you to resent me for...'

Her eyes blazed as she stared at him. She threw the cutlery on the table and leapt off her chair.

'You leave my parents out of this!' she shouted.

'Well, we have to confront our problems. It is not fair for us to live like this,' Robert said in firm but concerned tone of voice.

This angered her even more. She flew into a temper tantrum, picked up her plate and flew the contents into Robert's face. He was shocked and remained sitting there motionlessly without emotion. He was hurt. His heart was fractured into a myriad of fragments.

'Do not ever bring up my parents ever again!' she screamed at the top of her voice.

'I hate you!' she shouted in anger.

Roberts felt a dagger piercing through chest at that moment, experiencing the pain transmitted by every single sensory neurone, all at once, but all separate as well — in slow motion. As he sensed his heart breaking into at least a million pieces, it distressed him to wonder at that very moment whether it was at all reparable.

Margot's anger exploded even more, and she ran over to him with a book and began beating him repeatedly over the head. Rob just sat there motionless, all the while frozen in emotional turmoil. Not even a wink as he also mentally crashed. He felt himself sinking into a deep darkness, so much so that he was only able to recognise the faded outlines of the physical objects in the world around him.

Margot stopped suddenly when she realised that Rob was sitting there motionlessly without even a blink. There were tears rolling down his cheek with increasing momentum of regret. She was overwhelmed with regret and sadness herself and she ran out of the room. This was indeed the low-point of her psyche. A place she did not quite know how to ever resurface from.

Robert sat still on his chair for about a while searching for the strength to go to bed. He managed to make it, after some time, to his bedroom — broken in every possible way.

Chapter 8
Dances with Heaven and Hell

The day that a king has the courage to see himself in the eyes
of a beggar and the beggar has the opportunity to see himself
in the eyes of a king, the world would be a peaceful place to
live

Delhi, June 21, 1986 — The sky was cloudless and painted
with a shade of blue that was, above all, faultless. The ground
temperature at the newly-named, Indira Gandhi International
Airport was a sizzling thirty-four degrees Celsius. As Robert
emerged from the private jet, the light cool breeze he expected
across his already flushed face was noticeably absent.
However, the difference in the atmosphere was palpable. The
humidity was uncomfortably high and the heat was almost
intolerable. Parked and waiting at the bottom of the stairs of
the aircraft, were several black luxury vehicles, on stand-by, to
take Robert and his entourage to their luxury hotel.

As expected, he was physically drained after a sixteen-
and-half hour race across the sky, covering eight thousand
miles, or thereabouts. He hardly got a decent rest on the
journey, as he used most of his time to peruse through stacks
of documents in preparation for the meetings he had scheduled
on the following day. Despite his exhaustion, he curiously

peered through the window of his vehicle as it made its way into the city.

He was amazed at the infrastructure of the city, far more than he ever imagined he would. They passed by a queue of skyscrapers along the road waiting ever so patiently to win his attention. But what enthralled him the most, more so here than any other place he had been, were the rich characteristics of the people that he saw. He did not have to try very much to notice them, as they were in abundance and appeared deeply immersed in their jobs as they went about their daily activities. This was a most impressive sight to the billionaire in the back seat of the car.

As the car travelled through the crowded narrow streets in the heart of the city, the richness of colours leaping out before him were overwhelming. It spoke a language of its own. A language of contentment and happiness, of hard-work and dedication and of amiability and honesty. The very qualities that a make a businessman's pulse race with opportunity and excitement.

What was also overwhelmingly interesting to the curious foreigner, was the sharp visible contrast noticeable within this vibrant eastern city. Only a mere few yards separated skyscrapers from areas of squalor, the rich from the poor, the haves with the have-nots. But mind you, the lines of separation were quite distinct. Although this was arguably a feature of most modern cities at the time, it was strikingly more noticeable here. Despite this, the common denominator here was that it was populated by generally compliant, obliging and accommodating folks.

As the car moved further along, the richness of the country's religious and cultural heritage was evident.

Centuries of pride, innovation and tradition contributed to the backbone of this modern-day city. The architectural accomplishments highlighted the intelligence and talent of centuries of a rich and mature culture.

As the car pulled up in front of the hotel, there were several eloquently-attired men at the front, waiting in readiness to welcome the billionaire VIP. The back door of the vehicle was opened by one of the men, as the others stood waiting in a well-practiced, orderly queue with utmost respect and servitude.

'Welcome to India!' the man said, as Robert emerged from the car. 'Welcome to the Maharaja Hotel, sir. My staff and I are here to attend to you and your guests every need.'

'Thank you so kindly.'

The men immediately approached the other vehicles of Robert's entourage and proceeded immediately to take care of their luggage. Robert, accompanied by his team of bodyguards, was escorted through the impressively carved wooden main doors leading to a large marble lobby, the size of a playing field, by a modest estimation. It was all white and shiny, dazzling with the reflected light from the magnificent chandeliers suspended from the sky-high ceiling. If there ever was an image of heaven in the mortal world, it was unlikely to appear very much different.

He was led along the seemingly endless hallway towards an immaculately-dressed gentleman in a black three-piece suit and well-polished black shoes. His hair was short and neatly groomed. He stood upright, with a poised not dissimilar to a soldier on parade.

'Mr Lancaster, I am Mr Thackhur, the head concierge at the Maharaja. I would like to take the pleasure to welcome you here as our extraordinary guest of honour.'

'It is certainly my pleasure to be here in this great country and at such a magnificent hotel. It is most impressive,' replied Robert to the tall gentleman.

'Sir, may I take this opportunity to discuss a few pertinent details with you?'

'Sure, please go ahead,' instructed Robert.

'Sir, your absolute safety here is our top priority. In order to ensure this, I will like to offer you the services of our top security agents. They will serve to complement your security team to ensure your safety.'

Robert quickly replied that this was completely unnecessary. But the gentleman instead insisted — warning him.

'There is a lot about this country that your men would not know. Please accept my humble offer,' he pleaded with the foreign businessman.

Robert decided to accept Mr Thackhur's offer but insisted that they not to interfere with the work of his security team.

When he got to his room, the presidential suite, on the sixty-fourth floor, he found that the room was well-equipped with every luxury he had grown to become accustomed to. The generous view from his window was impressive as it surveyed the perimeter of the city, where the boundaries between the concrete jungle and the galvanised-covered huts of the surrounding slums were sharply demarcated. As he surveyed the view, Robert wondered of all the stories that were being acting out there and then, at that very moment in time, in both these opposing worlds and whether any of these would ever surface — into the other world.

Despite the air-conditioning system in his suite doing its best to triumphantly conquer the harsh, hot and humid weather conditions outside, as Robert opened the large window, reality rushed in. A hot wind blew onto his face forcing him to terminate that experiment of his, as swiftly as he could. He saw more sense then, in pouring himself a drink of whisky instead and sat down on the comfortable sofa next to the window. He laid back and allowed the release of his exhaustion into the milieu of a city that seemed ever so accommodating and obliging.

He opened his briefcase and started studying some documents in preparation for his meeting over dinner that evening with the principal of a prestigious institution. However, his keen passion for work was eventually defeated by his exhaustion and he soon fell asleep unintentionally. When he was eventually awoken, he realised that he was torpified for a good hour or so. It was four-thirty in the afternoon and the atmosphere outside was inviting. He had a quick shower and got into his casual clothes, intending to go out for a short walk to explore this interesting city. Adventure beckoned.

As Robert entered into the lobby on his way out, the stewards and stewardesses were clearly excited to see the billionaire in flesh and blood. However, to them, it was unusual for such a person to be seen wearing such casual clothes and to walk out into the world outside without any expectation of recognition. They thought that he was very much down to earth in his mannerism and attitude.

Accompanied by two of his bodyguards and trailed by a hotel security agent, Robert stepped out of the hotel into a world that was ripe for exploration and adventure. He soon rudely found out that the weather was a bit harsher than it appeared from inside the hotel. But he did not mind. It was not long before he could feel the sunshine attempting to burn its way through the skin of his forearm and a layer of sweat building up on his skin. Any pain he experienced was quelled by the kind of euphoria that sunshine usually attracts.

After walking about three blocks, he excitedly studied the multifactorial features that gave this place its uniqueness, while revelling in the joys of adventure that walking along the streets of a strange place offered. Just then, his curiosity was aroused by the nearly audible tinkling of bells. He walked loyally towards to the musical chimes. As he made his way further along the roadside, the sound grew louder and became more and more audible. The tinkling of the bells now had the tune of a symphony of metallic tunes. As he got even closer, he uncovered that the sound of the musical bells was accompanied by singing in a foreign language. This was interrupted periodically by the loud clanging of a metallic object.

He kept following the music until he reached a point on the pavement along the main street, where the sounds appeared to emanate from a place down a slope off the side of the street. He did not stop. He kept up his pursuit and proceeded left, trekking down a fairly steep slope. At the bottom, he looked up and noticed that the street was now at mountain-height above him. The sounds grew louder and Robert proceeded loyally towards it, guided only by his naked curiosity. He descended a flight of make-shift stairs down to a mud track that meandered through the tall grasses. The sound intensified.

At the end of the mud track, he found the sanctuary where the multi-tonal music was being given life. The music, now quite loud, was generated by cymbals and drums, punctuated by tinkling bells and the clanging of a metallic disc with a wooden hammer. No one noticed him as all the participants were standing, eyes closed, hands clasped and singing at the top of their voices, releasing the tensions of the day that had just gone by.

At the front of the audience, there was a large idol of a god sitting on a throne, protected by the large wide heads of beautifully painted cobras, standing at attention at the back of the idol. The idol was adorned with heaps of fresh flowers, money and fresh fruits. The gentleman at the front, dressed in a traditional outfit of a cloth wrapped around his waist and legs and wearing a necklace of beads, was worshipping the idol, using an earthen lamp crowned with a flame while chanting a hymn. The devotee circled the entirety of the idol in a clockwise, circular motion with the flame from the earthen lamp.

Robert advanced forward into the crowd, to share in the experience of the potent energy created by the chants at this secluded site within the heart of this busy city. As he looked to his left, he saw another anomalous guest, besides himself. Although it appeared that this individual had the strong passion for the chant, as much as any other person in the gathering that evening, he obviously did not belong there.

The young boy, not more than about five years of age, stood there, eyes closed, hands respectfully clasped and was chanting along passionately. He was wearing a set of dirty clothes that had obviously seen better times. It was probably reasonable to surmise that they were once white. They were also oversized and he appeared very unkempt. Although he had a most beautiful dark complexion, his face was stained with a soot-like powder. His lips appeared parched, eyes dull and sunken, and his cheek and collar bones prominent by default. His hair was a natural black, long and uncombed.

The young boy opened his eyes after the chanting was over, like everyone else. He stole a chance to gaze towards Robert, where their eyes met one another's. Robert's stare was intense, reciprocated by his observer. Robert saw a neglect, fright, hunger and loneliness in the eyes of the boy. Despite this, they were somehow filled with passion, determination and strong will.

"Perhaps he belongs to one of the labourers here in the audience," he hoped.

Robert started advancing slowly towards the boy, but this did not prove as easy as it should have been. The men in the crowd had come to notice the foreigner in their midst and had begun to surreptitiously talk about him with their acquaintances in a foreign language. Robert could have done without this unwanted attention. When the boy realised that Robert had noticed him, he quickly tried to move further and further away to avoid him.

Robert could not help it any longer. He turned to one of the men and asked, 'Excuse me. Do you know the young boy over there?'

Unfortunately, not many of the folks there understood or spoke much English. However, one gentleman came forward, flashing a warm, friendly and respectful smile at Robert, 'He is one of those kids... you know... one of them,' as he made some gesturing movements with his hands.

'Is he here with his parents today?' asked the foreign businessman.

'No, Sir. He is one of them... how do you say it... hmmm... homeless children. There are thousands of them in this city...'

At that point, Robert heard hustling footsteps behind him. As Robert turned around, he saw one of his bodyguards accompanied by a tall Indian gentleman in a Nehru suit.

'Sir, oh, there you are!' said his bodyguard faithfully. 'We have been looking everywhere for you. We lost you somewhere along the main street!

'Sir, you really must not wander off on your own like this. It makes it difficult for us to protect you!' the bodyguard politely scolded his boss.

Robert was just about to reply when he noticed that the young boy was slipping away. He was obviously, hoping to do so, unnoticed.

'Gentlemen, thank you so much. Please do me a kind favour and stay here. Wait for me here, I will be right back!' he told his men.

Robert walked off in pursuit of the child. He tried to be as surreptitious as possible in order not to intimidate or to scare the boy. After a few hundred yards, he called out to the child,

'Hey, I am Rob, do you mind if.'

The boy turned around and started running when he saw Rob chasing after him. Rob thought that he had no option now but to run after the boy. The boy ran faster and faster, so much so that Rob could barely catch up. He found himself approaching the arches of a massive bridge, above which the sound of a passing train was barely audible.

Suffering a bout of severe exhaustion, Rob decided to hide behind one of the pillars of the bridge. From there he could see the boy entering into the large space of one of the underground arches where he disappeared. After five minutes or so, Rob carefully threaded forwarded and peered inside. It was the most heart-breaking and shocking sight he had ever seen in his life.

Chapter 9
Dances with Conscience

Fortune is a great gift. Misery is a great opportunity. One cannot appreciate one without experiencing the other

As Robert Lancaster stood hiding behind a large concrete pillar, underneath a massive bridge in Delhi, his attention was interrupted by the rude buzzing from the relatively cumbersome cream-white device in his right hand. He pressed a button on the concave side of his cellular phone.

'Hello?' he answered in a whisper.

'Sir, I am sorry to disturb you but I just wanted to courteously remind you of your meeting with the principal in forty-five minutes.'

Robert looked at his watch and decided that he had to leave in hurry. He rushed back through the track he had previously trekked and found himself back to the place where the idol of the god was resting peacefully after a long day. The arena was now empty. The worshippers had left and the god appeared to be contented with the devotion bestowed upon it during the day.

There, he found that his security team was standing eagerly awaiting his return. Although they were happy having him return safely, they were obviously not very pleased about his impulsive adventure. They accompanied him up onto the main street where a black vehicle, with tinted windows, was parked on the side of the road waiting for him. He made it back to the hotel in minutes, rushed to his suite, had a shower and got ready for dinner with his guest of honour.

There was a heavy security presence in the VIP restaurant at the Maharaja, where Robert was due to meet the Honourable Professor Shankara, the principal of the most prestigious technology institute in India. Robert was led to a private room within the restaurant by his staff as he awaited the arrival of his guest.

A few minutes later, the door opened and the principal entered. Robert stood up and greeted him with clasped hands, congruent with the local custom.

'Professor Shankara, what an honour it is to finally meet you.'

'On behalf of the people of this great nation, I have the pleasure of welcoming you to our country.'

With pleasantries out of the way, the principal wasted no time in delving into the business of the evening. He outlined the great potential for expansion of the microcomputer industry in India and the significant impact this would have for his country.

'Mr Lancaster, you may well know that this country's greatest resource is its people,' he told Robert.

'We have one of the largest cohorts of talented individuals in computer technology in the world here, and we are working hard to further develop this industry here,' the principal said. 'Therefore, perhaps in the not-too-distant future, this country could well be poised for hosting a microcomputer company like yours.'

Robert agreed wholeheartedly, based on the research he had carried out. In fact, he was seriously considering this, hence his visit. The principal went on to outline the ambitions of the government in developing their intention of making India one of the superpowers of the world, which Robert was delighted to hear about and keen to be part of. However, he could not help but to interrupt his guest mid-sentence at one point, to ask a question. The sight Robert witnessed shortly ago, under the bridge, weighed heavily on his mind and this left him extremely unsettled.

'Professor, I was out having a walk this evening when I came across a group of children who appeared homeless. Is that something that is common here?'

He did not intend to be rude or inappropriate by asking this question, but what he observed under the bridge that evening burdened his conscience.

'Mr Lancaster, tell me — which country does not have issues such as this? No country is perfect; everywhere, there are problems such as this.'

'Is there anything that could be done to help?' asked the business executive.

'Our government have tried all sorts of tactics to combat the problem. We have tried to take them to orphanages but they prefer to live on the streets. It is impossible really!' answered the principal without an ounce of emotion.

'But, let us not get side-tracked here, Mr Lancaster,' the principal retorted.

But Robert insisted on changing the topic and this irritated his guest.

'I have come here to discuss the fate of India's most talented, some of the finest in the world, and here you are only interested in the "untouchables" — kids with no homes and no future. Do you think these kids could help your business in any way, Mr Lancaster?' the tall heavily-built man asked Robert firmly.

Robert paused for a moment and then lifted his head and apologised.

'I am sorry, perhaps, I may have gotten a bit side-tracked. Let's get back to business,' said Robert in a superficial, unenthusiastic tone of voice. His guest immediately agreed and they went on to talk about opportunities for the graduates to be interviewed and employed at Robert's highly prestigious computer firm in the United States.

After dinner, when all the business deals were more or less settled, Robert retired to his suite and sat down sipping on a glass of whisky. The sight he experienced under the arch of the bridge played in mind over and over again, as he recollected what he saw there.

As he hid behind the massive, tall pillar, he noticed the little boy running into the arch. The floor was blackened by soot, punctuated by water puddles throughout. The boy was not alone. There were countless others like him in that dark hall of hell. Most of them appeared to have already settled down to sleep. It looked as if the fortunate ones each had a small sheet of cardboard, which looked tired from over-use over time. Most of them, who were visible, appeared not to be as fortunate though and their tender, fragile bodies were left to be comforted and cushioned from the bare, partially moist, concrete floor, by the minimal tattered pieces of shredded cloth which they treasured as clothes. For some, this was their sole worldly possession.

As the boy walked in, they might as well had been fellow passers-by in New York City, for no one even acknowledged the other. Apparently, camaraderie was barely existent. If it was though, it was not obvious. This is not as surprising as one would think. They were all just kids. Life had not even had the chance to teach them the basics of human behaviour before throwing them into the abyss of human existence. The only behavioural pattern that they could afford was survival. In this harsh environment, unfortunately, most would not survive.

The poor boy's lips were parched and his stomach scaphoid in contour. Robert wondered to himself whether the boy had had anything to eat before retiring for the evening. How many of the others, there that evening, were also going to sleep with rumbling stomachs? They were likely to survive the night only because of thinking that tomorrow is not far away, and hopefully, it may be better.

Robert stood there, not only weeping with sorrow, but questioning how a kid of that age could develop the magnitude of strength and courage to look forward to another day. Another day of only another chance to fight for life at its lowest rung.

"What else have these kids experienced to make so tough and determined?" he asked himself, not really expecting or wanting to get an answer to that question.

The behaviour and attitude towards life and others at any random point in any individual's life is the sum average of their experiences before that index point. He shuddered at the thought that it was even possible that hell could be even worse.

"Not much worse though," he thought, reassuring himself, somewhat.

As he looked on, the boy disappeared from view and reappeared after a few minutes with a piece of treasure in his hand — his mattress — a torn, dilapidated piece of cardboard with the paper layers struggling to stay together. He carried it effortlessly, as it had lost the majority of its weight with time because of over-use.

He was about to spread the cardboard onto the concrete floor when he noticed that a young girl about his age, wearing an extensively stained and torn cotton dress, was about to lie on the bare concrete not far from his spot. Her soiled face was a clear reminder of many months of hardship and lack of love. He picked up his only possession and walked over to her and stared caringly at her.

The girl looked up and stared back at him with similar warmth. No words spoken. None needed. The little boy placed his cardboard mattress adjacent the girl, turned around and then returned to his previous spot. The girl slowly got up and moved over onto the cardboard before settling down to sleep.

Robert had now just finished sipping on his whisky from an exquisitely hand-crafted crystal glass and was about to go to bed. He got off the comfortable sofa and looked around. He felt a bit hungry as he had not much at dinner. On the table in front of him was a large bowl of fruits, none native to India. Each type was imported from a different part of the world. He picked up a juicy red apple and bit into it. It did not taste very good. It tasted of guilt. The guilt that filled his conscience from the sight he witnessed earlier that evening.

He had a shower and got into his pyjamas, ready for bed. As he sat down over the edge of the super king-sized bed, the mattress felt just perfect and inviting. He could not settle down though. He went to his personal lounge, within his suite, and had a glass of cold water. He tried to go back to sleep, but still could not.

He went back to the sofa and sat there listless in deep thought. He needed to off-load the burden that he was carrying before he could retire for the night, and before he could welcome the new day which laid ahead. Robert was a great believer in that there was a solution for every problem in life. You just have to look carefully. The answer was often not that far away.

Just then, the phone in his luxury hotel suite rang.

'Hello, Robert Lancaster.'

'Hi Dad, how are you doing?' It was Oscar, his son.

Oscar was now a law student at Oxford University. Although, he did not enjoy the closest of relationships with his father, they both kept in touch with each other through phone calls every now and again. Not as often as Robert would have preferred.

'Just been thinking that I haven't heard from you for a bit now,' said Robert.

'I have been pretty busy of late, preparing for my end of year finals. But all is well here. How about you?' the younger Lancaster asked.

'I am here on a short business trip,' Robert replied, 'I will be interviewing some very talented young people tomorrow and I am hoping to change theirs and others' lives forever.'

'When are you getting back to California?' asked Oscar.

'I may have to extend my visit a bit as there is something that has piqued my interest here.'

Oscar knew how savvy a businessman his father was and therefore, did not see any need to question him any further. He knew that he enjoyed planning the perfect business strategy.

But what he probably did not appreciate then was that his father had a passion for giving people a chance especially those that may not have had a fair one. Although he was good businessman, he was also a champion of the less fortunate.

Robert's mind was busy, even during the conversation with Oscar. He was still overly preoccupied with the homeless kid he had discovered, merely hours before. He picked up the phone and made a final call before retiring to bed. Following this, he was a tiny bit happier. He had worked out the outline of a clever plan in his head. This finally gave him the satisfaction he needed to calm his overactive conscience. He then managed to succumbed to his fatigue and went to bed.

The following morning, his security detail went into panic mode as he did not turn up in the VIP lounge for breakfast at seven a.m., as expected. He was not one to be late or absent. Kidnappings and abductions for ransoms were not unheard of in that part of the country. An immediate check of his suite compounded the panic as he clearly was not there. Calls to his cell went unanswered. Hotel security and the police were informed. All hell then broke loose.

Chapter 10
Dances with Angels and Demons

'When there is nothing to hold on to, nothing to rely on,
nothing to look forward to… there is always hope'

Robert's eyes were widely opened at four thirty in the morning. As the new day was waiting to be anointed by the warm rays of the tropical sunrise, Robert readied himself hastily. Dressed in a casual outfit, he left the hotel stealthily. He carried a bag filled with fruits and snacks, in addition to all the foodstuffs he could have mustered up from his suite. There was an eerie silence in the hotel at that hour, as he walked through the lobby unnoticed. Outside the main door, the calmness before the storm of all the bustling activities of the coming day was palpable in the air.

Fortunately, he did not come across many people as he trekked along the street towards the bridge, as being a middle-aged Caucasian, he would have surely would stand out like a sore thumb in that environment. Armed solely with determination and a torch, he proceeded down the steps off the road, through the mostly dark track, heading towards the arch under the bridge.

The ray of light from the torch illuminated the bowels of this modern city, shedding light on the dereliction of this capitalist society. It laid bare the exigency for a ray of hope, desperately needed, to extinguish the flames of his overstimulated conscience particularly, as he had been a witness to this travesty. Lying on the cold, bare floor, was a plethora of bodies, all in haphazard orientations, some covered and others not so fortunate to be. It depicted a grave of humanness and exposed the apathy of a society for those who have fallen through the cracks of life at such a tender age. They were too young to even ponder why it had to be them.

The light sparked a dramatic reaction from the kids sleeping on the floor. They sprang up from their sleep with borrowed energy, leapt on their feet and ran with all the might they could summon. Realising that the light from the torch had startled and scared the kids off, Rob switched it off promptly. Unfortunately, this was already beyond the point of 'no return'. In the flurry of activities, he did not have much of a chance to find the little boy from the previous day. It did not matter because he now realised that the boy was one of many; he was but a drop of water in this sea of human tragedy and despair.

'Stop, stop, stop!' he screamed at the absquatulating kids. I am not going to hurt you!

'Stop, please stop!

'I have brought you something to eat,' he shouted in vain, because by this time, the arch was already empty.

His attempts at reassuring the kids or getting them to comply were completely futile. It was obvious that it would take a lot more than this to convince the kids that he was there just to offer help and did not pose a danger to them.

At first, the reaction of the kids to his presence did not quite make sense to the businessman. He just wanted to offer them something to eat. This act of kindness was never before experienced by the kids in that way and hence, they reacted instinctively and ran away.

"They all must be starving," he thought. "Why would they just run off like this? It was like I was some sort of monster to them."

He then thought how difficult it must be for these kids. The emotional trauma they face each and every day must be overwhelming.

"How do they summon the strength and courage to survive?" he questioned himself.

He placed the bag on the floor and leaned on the dirty brick wall of the arch as his body slid down in sheer frustration. He was able to reassure himself and his conscience with the thought that, he at least he tried, but then felt personally compelled to do more. What or how could he do to win the trust of these kids — were questions that he did not quite have the answers to that morning.

He sat there for close to an hour in deep contemplation, until the rays of sunlight began to dispel the darkness of the night. He felt the longing for a cup of hot coffee to comfort himself. Robert stood up and steadied himself, and then slowly walked up the path he had come down, back to the other side of the world. The world where folks do not have to worry about all the travesties of the battleground under the bridge.

As he negotiated up the path towards the main street, he began hearing the sounds of cymbals, then bells… and then the most beautiful melody of a hymn that the locals were chanting in front of the altar off the side of the street. He followed the sounds again to the open space temple where the god resided.

He stood behind the crowd of devotees, who, no matter who they were, all added their humble voices to produce the most soul-warming choral Rob had ever heard. He took it all in, feeling like a cheat, as he was unable to contribute. But like the others, he clasped his hands and stood there with his eyes closed. The bliss it brought him lifted his spirits in an indescribable and incredible way.

The end of the chant was marked with the loud and powerful sound of the lead devotee blowing into a large snail's shell. 'What a mind-blowing performance this was,' Rob surmised. As he opened his eyes, he saw the little boy, from the evening before, standing just a few metres from him. He was wearing the same dirty and torn clothes with dried lips. He was so thin that his ribs were noticeably visible though the tears in his shirt. His limbs were stick-like and barely thick enough to support even his miniature frame.

As their eyes met, he turned around in a deep fear and hastily negotiated his way through the small crowd disappearing in the wilderness of the city. Although Robert wanted to chase after him, he did not this time, as he had to make it back to the hotel to get on with the business of the day. He went back on foot, as he had come when the day was a bit younger and the city was far less bustling.

At the front of the hotel there were several police vehicles with a flurry of policemen at the entrance. Up above, a helicopter was rotating repeatedly. Despite the obvious sight and sound of possible existing danger, Robert walked calmly up to the front entrance and entered the premises.

Calvin Rodriguez, Robert's head of security, rushed over to him.

'Sir, are you all right?'

'Where have you been? We feared that the worst had happen to you!'

'Calvin, what is all of this unnecessary drama about?' demanded Robert.

'First of all, sir, are you all right?' he asked his boss, for the second time.

'Yes, of course!' Robert retorted, as he was a bit irritated at the commotion that his brief absence had created. 'I simply woke up early and went for a walk.'

'Sir, that is absolutely fine, but I would have preferred if you had let me know about this,' Calvin said. 'We can't protect you if we are kept in the dark about your whereabouts!'

Robert was also fuming by now, but simply walked off to his suite to get prepared for the rest his day. He had a shower and got dressed. He walked over to the dining table, picked up a knife and an apple. He decisively sliced the apple into several pieces and devoured it along with a hot brew of coffee which already placed ready on the table for him.

At eight a.m. sharp, there was a knock on the door to indicate that his security detail was all ready to escort him to the university. The interviews for computer and IT engineers where due to take place there. On the ride over, Robert was handed a file of a summary of the candidates who were appearing for the interviews that day. He placed it aside, as his concentration was more fixated on life on the streets of this busy city.

He noticed that, mingled amongst the bustling workers in a rush either trying to get to work or already working, there were kids similar to the little boy from under the bridge, negotiating their way through the passers-by on the pavements. They physically appeared filthy, with worn and torn clothes, no footwear to protect the soles of their feet against the heat of the asphalt covered streets. Their presence mustered not as much as a glance from the passers-by. He got the feeling that these kids did not have a shred of a safety net in their lives nor received any compassion from the surrounding people, who were mostly indifferent to their needs and vulnerabilities.

As the car stopped at the traffic lights at an intersection, Robert noticed a young girl about five or six years of age rummaging through the garbage bin on the corner of the street, searching for an ounce of nutrition to sustain the body that hosted her overactive determination for survival. A few metres away, separated only by a glass window, well dressed patrons were feasting on bowls of hot soup, in plain sight of the world.

He arrived at the university fifteen minutes before the start of the interviews. He and his team were immediately directed to the main interview hall. Already there, waiting to greet them, was Professor Shankara.

'Mr Lancaster, welcome to the finest campus for technology in all of India and possibly all of Asia. We welcome you to our place,' said Professor Shankara with a booming voice.

'Thank you, Professor,' replied Robert.

'It was only this morning that I was thinking what a great day it was going to be. Soon, you will have some of the brightest computer minds in the world, working in your great company and in return, this would give so many of my students a chance of a lifetime, to work for such a prestigious entity,' boasted the professor.

They all sat down, taking their seats around the large boardroom table. Robert was seated at the head of the table and surrounded by the other senior personnel of his company from California. They included the head of technological operations and the head of human resources. Also sitting on the interview panel was Professor Shankara.

As they all settled down on their respective seats, Robert turned to his PA on the right.

'Is Norman here as yet?'

'No sir, he is due in early tomorrow morning', she replied.

'Are we missing someone?' asked Professor Shankara.

'No, Professor, we can carry on with the interviews today, but we will have to wait until tomorrow for my colleague, Mr Fitzgerald, to arrive before we could appoint the successful candidates,' replied Robert.

'And what exactly is this, Mr Fitzgerald's, role in this process?' asked the professor, rather impatiently.

'Norman is my head legal advisor and is going to bring in the contracts for signing. He has been working hard on this whilst we have been here. I called him last night and we had a chat about this.'

The professor then nodded in agreement.

Norman Fitzpatrick was one of Rob's best friends. He was one, of the only two people, that Robert would trust with his own life. The other was Alan Shugard, his previous business partner. Robert had known Norm for many years. He was one of the unsung greatest legal minds at Stanford University, whilst Rob was a student there. Although, Norman had fought hard for Rob to remain in the law program there, he met with stiff opposition from his colleagues at the time. Robert turned to him for legal advice when he formed his first company with Alan, and soon afterwards, employed him in his firm. He has remained a loyal friend to Rob ever since.

At nine a.m. sharp, the first candidate was summoned into the interview room. Professor Shankara introduced Robert and the team and then handed over to him. Robert took the opportunity to expound on the great opportunity that laid ahead. He then handed over to the various members of the team, who went through the candidate's achievements and abilities in great detail. Rob elected to ask the final few questions. The interview then started.

'Mr Manu, what is the greatest lesson that life has taught you so far?'

The young genius was taken aback by the question and was one he certainly was not prepared for. He fumbled spectacularly and unfortunately, was not able to formulate a decipherable response.

'Okay then, if I were to give you a million dollars this minute, what would you do with it?'

'With the money?' asked the now trembling candidate.

'With the money, your life or anybody else's,' replied Rob. 'It is an open question.'

Again, the young man looked completely lost and bewildered at Rob's line of questioning. Tears began welling up in his eyes.

'Can I ask you a final question?' Rob asked.

The young man nodded in agreement.

'What do you see as the most pronounced problem in the world around you right now, and if you could do something about it, what would you do?'

'Sir, I have worked hard all my life for an opportunity like this. I have never thought about having great sums of money before and how to spend it, or about the problems of the world. What I know about best of all, is about computer software programming and if I were given a chance to work for you, I promise to work very hard to the best of my ability.'

Robert thanked him and informed him that a final decision would be made at the end of all the interviews.

Professor Shankara was surprised by Rob's questions as he expected more technically-related ones. So, he asked Robert about the reasons for his line of questions. Rob simply flashed a wry smile at him.

Robert asked each candidate the same aberrant questions; all were taken by surprise but some were able to reply, a few of whom even impressed the CEO with uncut, raw and brutal honesty in their responses. This was all deliberate, as there was much to more to a person than their professional abilities: like how human they were.

The interviews went on all day and finished at ten in the evening. By the end of it all, Robert knew exactly who he wanted to appoint. He waited for the list of successful candidates that the panel had put forward and he added a few more based on the answers he had to his bespoke questions. This attracted some disagreement from the professionals around the table as they thought those selections were unjustifiable but, in the end, the CEO's decisions were not challengeable.

Robert instructed that the successful candidates from the interview were to be divided amongst the panel members to contact in person the following morning. He produced a list of about fourteen names and asked that Norman, himself, contacted these the following morning.

'Sir, do you think that Mr Fitzpatrick the best person to do this?' the head of human resources asked.

'Why not?' asked Robert, as this was all part of a plan he had hatched the night before.

There was a look of disagreement in her eyes but she accepted his decision.

'Please let me know as soon as Norm arrives?' he asked, as he prepared to leave.

Chapter 11
Dances with Light and Darkness

To conquer life, one must conquer fear

Robert got back to the hotel accompanied by his security detail. He was quite tired after an intense day but fatigue never slowed him down before. As he was about to enter his suite, he beckoned Calvin over to ask for his help.

'I would like to let you know something. I am planning to visit a site under the city's iconic bridge about half a mile from here. I would like to take some food along with blankets. Can you arrange to muster up these items for me please?' he asked in a low voice.

'How much and what kinds of food and how many blankets, sir?'

'As many blankets and as much food as we could physically carry.'

'When do you need these for, sir?', asked Calvin rather confused.

'Tonight!' Rob replied.

'Sir, I do not know what is going on or for whom these are for, but you must know that going over there at such a time is simply not safe,' Calvin warned him.

'I will take my chances, Calvin,' he replied, 'But please do not make a great scene about it this time!' Rob said, raising his voice a bit.

'Sir, I cannot allow you to do this on your own,' said Calvin firmly.

'What I am saying, sir, is that it is simply not safe. Maybe I should come along as well?' asked the bodyguard.

'That's fine with me Calvin, I don't mind. But what I don't want, is unnecessary attention about this, especially from the media!' Robert clarified.

'Sure, I understand sir'.

Robert had a quick shower and changed into a set of regular clothing, similar to that usually worn by the locals. He wore a pair of khaki trousers and an untucked, short sleeved, cotton shirt with thin light blue vertical stripes, together with a pair of white sneakers. He gobbled on a pastry and an apple as he awaited word from Calvin about the goods that he had requested.

Shortly afterwards, he received a phone call from his bodyguard to say that everything was ready. They both headed off, leaving the hotel discreetly. By then, as the time approached midnight, the heat had died down and the atmosphere was cooler and far more tolerable than earlier. As they walked towards the bridge, he felt a closer connection with the man who accepted the selfless job of putting his life at risk, to save him.

'Calvin, how is your family?' Rob asked, turning his head in Calvin's direction as they trekked along. 'I feel as if I should ask this question more often, but we rarely get a chance to chat like this,' he pointed out.

'They are fine, sir, thank you for asking. Ted is now five and Elena is six years old. They are both enjoying school. They are a bit of a handful for my wife at times, of course, but she is great with them.'

'Do you get to spend a lot of time with at all?' Rob asked.

'Not a whole lot, but enough, you know…' he replied.

They both carried on chatting for a bit, when Calvin decided to ask, 'May I ask, sir, why are going under the bridge at this time of the night?'

'Calvin, please call me Rob.

'You might not believe this, but despite the beauty of this city and the wonderful people here, I have uncovered one of its gravest problems. It is one that exists in other most cities but it is usually hidden from the view of the world. But here, it is not. It involves innocent homeless kids who have no other alternative but to live and survive on the streets. These boys and girls have not existed long enough to have developed the survival skills that they need in a ruthless world like this.'

Calvin was still a bit confused as to what his boss was actually trying to tell him, but more so, the reason both of them were trekking through the bowels of a strange city, in the middle of the night.

"Surely we are not like the superheroes depicted in various cartoons who fight away the problems of the world with their supernatural powers at nights and blend in with the ordinary during daytime hours," he thought to himself.

'I have found out that this city has more than an uncomfortable number of homeless kids who have no source of sustenance, or love, for that matter', said Robert. 'I will show you where they gather together and stay at nights, a place far from secure', said Robert to the tall, stern, well-built war veteran.

'I'm with you, Boss,' Calvin replied.

'That's great to hear Calvin. By the way, you may wish to acquire a cardboard or two to take along with you,' said Robert, turning towards to bewildered Calvin.

Robert took him down the path off the side of the road, towards the place Robert had come to regards as 'hell-on-earth', located under the bridge. As they approached the arch, Robert turned off his torch and instructed Calvin to do the same. Not long after the path ended, Rob guided Calvin to a small opening between the bushes that served as the doorway into the arch. The place was pitch dark, apart from the silhouettes of bodies on the floor before them. Calvin removed the massive knap-sack he was carrying filled with supplies and placed it quietly on the floor.

'What now, Boss?'

They both leaned onto the brick-wall and eased themselves down onto the floor. They did not have a cardboard to sit on. The floor was damp and cold.

'This, my dear Calvin, is the abyss of human existence,' muttered Rob quietly.

'What's the plan now?'

'Let's leave the supplies here for the kids. They will have something to eat in the morning when they wake up,' replied Rob. 'I am a bit shattered now. Can we rest for a minute or two before we head back?'

Calvin chuckled quietly.

They sat there for about ten minutes, when the silence of the arch was interrupted by deep and heavy male voices, emanating from somewhere outside. They were muttering in a foreign language. The noises grew louder relatively quickly. They now sounded as if they were close by now. The entrance of the men was preceded by rays of light rushing into the arch from heavy-duty torches.

Both Rob and Calvin were taken aback by this development.

"Who were these men coming here past midnight? Did they know that there were homeless kids sleeping there? What were their intentions?" wondered both gentlemen.

"Perhaps they were bringing food and necessities for the kids after all, like they were doing," wondered Robert.

As he looked up, the outlines of three burly men, wearing traditional Indian clothing, followed by a fourth in a khaki outfit with stripes on his sleeves. The gentleman at the back appeared to be a police officer. This was reassuring to both gentlemen, but unfortunately this reassurance survived in their minds only temporarily.

The men rushed onto the floor and grabbed hold of a kid each. The children were cruelly awoken by the monstrous grip on their tender and frail torsos. Their screeches of shock and fright were like an alarm that awoke the others from their sleep and served as the warning for them to run... to run as fast as their might would allow.

Robert and Calvin sprung unto their feet, and they both ran towards the sounds of the screaming kids. Robert leapt forward and threw his weight onto one of the men and they both went crashing onto the floor. He had the faint glance of a boulder within arm's reach. He quickly picked it up and pounded the head of the man till he fell unconscious onto the cold, damp floor.

One of the men ran off with a girl in his grips. Calvin chased after him in hot pursuit. He was fast but his athletic capabilities were no match for the well-built, muscular veteran Marine. Calvin soon caught up with him and thumped the living hell out of him with his bare hands. He rushed back to the arch in the darkness, afraid that his boss maybe in danger from the other crooks. With one hand, he held on to the little girl, he had just rescued, and the other to the collar of the miscreant, dragging him along the path covered in pebbles, many with sharp edges.

When he got back, he found that Robert was in complete control of the situation, comforting one of the kids who was crying uncontrollably. To the side of him was an unconscious man with blood seeping from a large laceration over his temple. There were a few other kids who had now returned and were surrounding his boss by then. The third villain and the policeman were nowhere in sight, as clearly, they had managed to escape.

'Are you all right, Boss?' asked Calvin

'Not bad… not bad at all. Thank you so much,' replied Rob. 'Let's get this sorted now and get these criminals to justice.'

Calvin used his belt to tie the wrists and ankles of the captured goon and then turned his attention to the little girl who had suffered a laceration on her forearm. He removed his shirt and ripped a strip off it to improvise as a tourniquet in order to stop the oozing from her forearm. He had a look at the abrasion that the little boy had on his temple and reassured him that all was fine.

In the meantime, Rob picked up his cellular phone, which he always kept with him, and phoned through to the hotel to speak to his security team. He decided not to inform the police initially as he wasn't sure whether it was the sensible thing to do or not, in view of one of the villains dressed in police uniform. He asked that his security team consult the Indian security officer assigned to his protection, as he would be more knowledgeable as to who to report the incident to. He also asked for urgent medical help.

Rob went over to the bag, opened it, and asked all the kids to have something to eat. Initially they were not so sure whether they could trust these foreigners, but their hunger dictated the outcome of their final decision. Rob brought over a pastry and an apple for the frightened little boy, who looked him directly in the eyes for several moments before weakly reaching out to have the apple. It was the same boy who he had noticed before at the altar.

Within ten minutes, sirens were heard wailing in the quietness night. The previous sleeping city was now turned into an amusement park of flashing red and blue lights. Rob and Calvin were walking around impatiently, waiting for the foot soldiers to arrive to deliver their catch of the night. When the police officers arrived, all the kids, including the rescued little boy and girl, ran away as fast they could. This was reminiscent of a reflex reaction, rather than a sensible or premeditated one. Both Rob and Calvin felt completely helpless and disappointed at that stage.

Shortly after the police arrived, the paramedics did as well, and they went over to the criminal lying flat out on the floor. They assessed him and bandaged his forehead. By that stage, the man had regained consciousness. He had lost a considerable volume of blood but not enough to have any lasting effect on his now regained physical state of consciousness.

The police proceeded to arrest both criminals and they marched them to the back of their vehicle. Some of the officers simultaneously interviewed both tourists.

'What were you doing here at this time of the night?' asked the inspector.

'I came along with Calvin, the head of my security detail, to bring over some food and essentials for these poor kids.'

'Was there not a more favourable time to do this deed of kindness?'

'I am here on business, sir. We came here after my work finished for the day,' replied a tired and frustrated Robert.

'Sir, forgive me for asking these questions, but it is not unusual for men like yourself to come here at night to kidnap these homeless kids here, to sell to high-paying clients from all over the world for various malicious reasons,' explained the inspector.

'Sir, I am a successful businessman. My business has nothing to do with exploiting homeless kids...' said Robert before he was interrupted by the policeman.

'Sir, you may say that, but I am having serious trouble understanding why any rational person would leave their bed and come over her in the wee hours of the morning for any other reason but malevolent ones!' asserted the police inspector.

'Sir, rational is a relative term,' exclaimed Robert. 'Similarly, I have trouble understanding why "rational" human beings would not come here every night to provide these kids with something to eat and a warm blanket even, at the very least!' thundered Robert, losing his patience.

Robert was soon to find out the police officers there did not quite like being shouted at, or challenged.

'Sir, I would need both of you to come down to the station, where you will be spending the rest of the night,' relayed the policeman in a calm tone of voice and walked off, unconcerned.

Much to Robert's concern however, two policemen walked over and placed handcuffs on both Robert and Calvin. Robert protested intensely but the policemen simply told them to save their protests and explanations for the next day, when they would be formally interviewed. They were both escorted to the back of another jeep and taken to the police station.

Chapter 12
Dances with Truth

'Truth is the building block of inner strength'

The billionaire's security team arrived at the scene shortly after the police managed to, but were barred from entering the arch under the bridge. Although this felt a bit shifty, as foreigners they felt as they were not well positioned to argue with the local law enforcement officers. They waited patiently instead, at the entrance, where an army of policemen were walking all around them, and some were even keeping a close eye on them as well.

They managed to catch a glimpse of the handcuffed criminals emerging from the entrance as they were escorted to the police jeep. Their imaginations ran wild as to what was going on and what had happened.

'Is my boss all right in there?' one of them questioned.

'Sir, please stand back. This is a crime scene. Please do not obstruct the police from doing our job!' exclaimed one of the officers.

'I am simply asking after the welfare of my boss who is in there, and is a victim in this heinous ordeal!'

A small team of policemen approached the foreigners and asked them again to move away to clear the entrance.

'This is a police order. Failure to comply would be interpreted as obstruction to justice!' they were sternly instructed.

Although they did not get a good feeling about this, they had no choice but to comply. They stood back and waited. They were shocked moments later when they got a glimpse of both their boss and Calvin, brandishing handcuffs around their wrists, being escorted to the back of a dingy police jeep. The policemen were being a bit heavy-handed with their suspects. The foreigners were paralysed in shock.

At the police station, the Americans were greeted by the angry chanting of an expanding, vibrant mob at the entrance, pelting slurs at the men in a language they could not comprehend. They were escorted into the building and taken straight to the interview room. Once there, Rob and Calvin were released from their handcuffs by an officer, who gave them both an unwelcoming stare.

'The Chief Commander will be with you soon,' he said as he left the room.

'What the hell is happening here?' asked Robert in a low but angry tone of voice as he turned towards Calvin.

'I don't get a good feeling about this, sir,' said the bodyguard. 'I think we are being set up.'

'Nonsense,' replied Robert. 'I am sure they know that we are innocent and once they've done their checks, they will let us go.'

'To be honest, sir, I'm not so sure,' replied Calvin in an unsettled tone of voice.

At that point the heavy metal door opened and much to their disbelief, an officer in uniform walked in with the poise and arrogance of inappropriate aristocracy. The surprising thing was that they had seen this gentleman before, even not so long ago, in fact… in the arch under the bridge. He was the police officer who accompanied the villains.

'When I walk into a room, everyone stands!' he shouted.

'Sorry, but who are you?' enquired Robert. 'Although we have seen each other only recently, we did not have a chance for introductions as you ran off before we could!'

'Shut up! Silence!' shouted the man, angrily. 'I am Chief Commander Muradali.

'You foreign gentlemen have come to my country to commit crimes and you will pay for it,' the commander warned, as he temporarily stopped pacing across the room and leaned over the table top to fix his eyes directly at Robert and Calvin.

Robert was uncontrollably upset at the thought of this high-ranking officer abusing the powers of his office from the recent events he bore eyewitness to.

'We are not criminals, you bastard!' shouted Robert uncontrollably as he leapt off his seat.

'What did you call me?'

Robert remained quiet, as he began to see the point Calvin was making earlier. He was however, unwilling to cooperate with this goon and needed to wait patiently to seek the assistance of someone with higher authority.

'I am going to bring in eyewitnesses, to confirm that you both were committing a devious crime,' he said.

'Gentlemen, here, in this country, we take these matters seriously!

'Bring in the witnesses to ID these criminals,' the commander ordered.

The door opened and three men entered. One had a thick bandage over his forehead, the other had generalised bruising over his face with an obvious deformity of his nose. The last one appeared untouched. As they entered, they began shouting loudly all together.

'Sir, these are the men who were trying to kidnap those innocent children under the bridge tonight,' said one of the men. 'This one was about to rape one kid,' pointing to Robert.

'They are evil! They need to be imprisoned,' said another. 'They were talking about capturing the kids to make a big sale in America.'

The commander, pretending that he was meeting the men for the first time, raised his head in a manner that would erase his sins and give himself and the others a renewed confidence in morality and justice.

'Gentlemen, you are both screwed! These men are all respected men in this country and the evidence they have been brave enough to give here tonight, is like gold,' he said, in a low but sustained voice.

'This is ludicrous...' started Rob, when the commander spoke hastily to his officers.

'Take them away. Now!' he thundered.

By this time the rest of Mr Lancaster's security had arrived at the police station, and they were immediately informed that the two men were charged and imprisoned for kidnapping and sexual offences to minors. They were also informed that the police were in possession of strong and reliable evidence.

Things looked grim for the foreigners. There was an unstoppable sense of coldness spreading from their extremities to the tightened muscles on their chest and on the back of their necks. This could not be right. They have known their boss and Calvin for many years and this was not at all congruent with who they were, what they stood for nor their behaviour.

"Calvin had kids of similar age for heaven's sake," they thought. "This just did not seem right."

In desperation, they decided to phone their Indian counterpart, Mr Sanjay Khan.

'Hello, who is this?' answered the low voice at the end of the line.

'Mr Khan, it is Pete. I am sorry to bother you this early in the morning, but we need your help urgently.'

'Don't be silly, I have already been awake for the last two hours and have finished my morning rituals and prayer, no need to apologise,' said Mr Khan. 'What is wrong. Tell me'.

'We have a serious situation. We are at the police station. Mr Lancaster and our head of security have been arrested and is currently in police custody,' said Pete Hardy.

'Oh, that is serious,' agreed Mr Khan. 'Why?'

They have been accused of kidnapping and sexual offences to minors,' relayed the American.

'Minors… who are these minors?'

'What I know is that, the plight of the homeless kids under the bridge has caught the interest of the boss over the last few days.'

'Were they there under the bridge when they were arrested?'

Pete thought that the answer to this question did not sound good and certainly did not make a good case for the accused men but he replied honestly.

'Yes'

'It all makes sense. Don't worry, I will need to make some calls,' Mr Khan said to the surprise of the foreigner.

'What do you mean? Are you going to come over?' asked Pete.

'Peter, I suspect that they have been set up. They are innocent. I will explain later,' he said. 'Do you have a lawyer?'

'Our chief lawyer is due to arrive here from California anytime now. He was summoned by the boss yesterday for a business-related matter.'

'Have him meet me as soon as he gets in, please!' instructed Mr Khan and the line went dead.

A few minutes later at 6.15 a.m., Pete had a call from the hotel to inform him that Norman Fitzpatrick had arrived. He arranged to meet him there in ten minutes and then placed a call to Mr Khan to inform him of Mr Fitzgerald's arrival.

'Mr Khan, the lawyer has arrived at the Maharaja Hotel from the States,' Pete told him. 'I am headed straight there, right now.'

'Okay, I will meet you there in a few minutes,' confirmed Mr Khan.

Ten minutes later, Pete made it into the Maharaja, closely followed by Mr Khan. They saw a tired-looking Norman Fitzpatrick pacing a corner of the lobby impatiently. He wore a double-breasted, tweed blazer fully-buttoned up. Pete had known the elderly gentleman after a few brief encounters at meetings in the past.

'Good morning, Mr Fitzpatrick,' said Pete as he approached the gentleman.

'Good morning. Where is Robert?' he asked impatiently, looking around. 'It is vital that I speak to him urgently before we go off into the meeting and before we appoint our new employees later this morning.'

'The boss is in prison,' he replied.

'In prison?' he asked in a raised, shocked tone of voice. 'What the hell is going on here?'

Pete took a minute to update Mr Fitzgerald and Mr Khan about the events of the last few hours. Both men were infuriated and agreed that something was not quite right. Mr Khan had several high-level contacts in the city and had easy access to privileged and classified information from these close contacts.

'For a long time, there has been a ring of child smugglers who operated in the underworld of the city,' he claimed. 'This ring is currently being run by high level officials who have managed to evade the law.'

'For Christ's sake, Robert, why did you have to get involved in this mess?' asked Norman rhetorically in an exasperated tone of voice.

Pete did not know all the facts, but indicated that the boss had developed a keen interest in this humanitarian exigency.

'I am able to unearth some valuable evidence of this ring and of the villains,' said Mr Khan, 'But I need your help, sir, to get Mr Lancaster out of prison.'

'We have to get to Robert and find out what he knows about this and see what evidence he could provide. I think this is priority here,' said the acclaimed lawyer.

'It is obvious that Mr Lancaster had unearth or witnessed something he was not meant to. Therefore, we need to hurry! They will try to get rid of him one way or the other,' Mr Khan pointed out.

Mr Khan went off to the telephone to make a call and came back soon afterwards. The three men then headed straight for the police station with Pete in control of the luxury four-wheeler, driving as fast as he could through the veins of the city, at its busiest time. They made slow but steady progress in the morning rush-hour traffic, and managed to get there in just under forty-five minutes.

The three men rushed into the station. To their surprise, there was a remarkable sense of calm in there, which was in stark contrast to the situation just a couple of hours before. It definitely was not in keeping with the excitement of the recent sequence of events or even with the general climate of the surrounding city. Something was fishy about it all.

'We would like to see Mr Lancaster, please?' asked Pete, speaking to the officer at the desk.

'I am sorry, we have no one here by that name,' he replied.

Mr Fitzpatrick, upon hearing this, straightened up as if he was struck by a bolt of lightning, waking him up like a fully-charged electric motor. He walked briskly towards the desk. He leaned over and spoke to the officer in a deep, loud tone of voice.

'I am only going to say this once. I am Norman Fitzpatrick. My client was arrested and brought here in the early hours of this morning. I would like to see him. Now!'

'Sorry, sir, you must be mistaken, we've had no prisoner here by that name here,' he said in a rushed, weak but determined voice.

Pete grew impatient at that point and leapt forward and lunged at the uniformed policeman behind the desk, before he was held back by Mr Khan. At that moment, another officer, obviously more senior, entered behind the counter to address the men. He looked squarely at Mr Khan and spoke to him.

'Mr Lancaster and his colleague were arrested in the early hours of today morning and it seems that they have been transferred out to a facility on the outskirts of the city,' he said.

'Where have they been transferred?' Norman demanded to know.

'Sir, this information, I cannot give you,' replied the officer firmly.

'As their lawyer, I demand to know. They are American citizens and they have rights,' shouted the veteran lawyer.

'Sir, with all due respect, this is India!' said the officer, shaking his head from side to side.

'This is not good,' whispered Mr Khan.

Chapter 13
Dances of the Knights

There is always a spark of light somewhere in the darkness.
You just have to look for it

The Americans were frustrated as they stood at the front desk of the local police station in Delhi city, knowing that their boss and chief bodyguard had been arrested, and without any warning, transferred away to an unknown destination. The police officers were not giving enough information for them to work on. With each passing second, they became increasingly worried about the safety of their fellow countrymen, in this foreign land.

Here in Delhi, under these particular circumstances, things were not as straight forward as they appeared. There were lots of irregularities in this story and, to compound the confusion, the local police were being quite shifty and unhelpful. What really was going on and why? The lawyer and the two senior security men were highly suspicious of foul play by the authorities.

Moment later, the sombre mood at the station was shattered with the deep, orotund voice of a tall gentleman who entered the station and stood directly behind the foreigners.

'Hmmm, hmmm,' he cleared his throat. This was unmistakably a command to everyone in the room to step aside to provide him with access, as he approached the officers at the front desk. He was dressed in a brown uniform with three stars on each side of his collar and a police cap with three stars on the visor. He flaunted a serious, unsmiling facial gesture, spectacles and a black thick moustache, the colour of which, was inconsistent with his age.

He looked at Norman and introduced himself.

'I am the Director General of Police here in Delhi, DGP Argarwal,' he said.

Norman looked at him and was about to introduce himself when he replied, 'I know who you are!'

As they spoke, there was a flurry of activities within the station. This involved an invasion of the station by truckloads of police officers from elsewhere. They appeared from behind the two policemen at the front desk and asked them to stand still. Surprisingly, both policemen were handcuffed and taken away.

'What is going on here, sir', asked Norman as he addressed the senior policeman.

'Please sir, let's go into the room at the back and I will explain,' DGP Agarwal requested.

Norman and Pete were a bit sceptical about this, but they received a nod from Mr Khan that hinted that it was probably safe to do so. They then, more confidently than before, followed DGP Argarwal into a large room within the station, where the senior policeman offered them all seats and then sat down beside them to explain.

'I know that you are all worried about your boss, Mr Lancaster,' he began. 'First of all, due to the intelligence we have gathered and the rapid response from my team, I can confirm that both gentlemen are safe and they are on their way back here. My orders!'

'Thank goodness!' exclaimed Norman. 'Why were they arrested?'

'They were wrongly arrested!' he said. 'We have been investigating a ring of child smugglers for years here in Delhi, but we've never had enough information or evidence to stop them... until last night' he explained.

'I am still a bit confused here,' admitted Norman.

'This ring of villains has been abducting homeless kids and selling them on the black market to international paedophiles and others who use them as slaves, or even used them as organ donors against their will. It is a real tragedy. Your boss and his bodyguard have given eyewitness accounts of this last night.'

'Oh dear! It still does not explain why they've had to go through this nightmare despite providing this valuable information to the police,' enquired Norman.

'Well, unfortunately this ring was run by several rogue policemen from this station and that's the reason they were charged and transferred out almost immediately. Had we not had the intelligence and intercepted the transfer of your boss from here, both of them would have been killed by now!'

This last statement sent shockwaves down the spine of Norman. He had only stepped out of a plane a few hours ago to attend to business matters. Little did he know what he about to face here in Delhi that morning. It was all unwanted excitement to him at this stage in his life.

'Imagine, one of the most prominent businessmen in the world being killed by these insignificant, useless goons in a strange land, only because he was touched by the plight of these unfortunate kids! What a travesty that would have been!' exclaimed Norman.

'In this country, we take our duties and responsibilities seriously, including those to the honest and hardworking citizens. It is unfortunate that there are some "rotten apples" in the midst, but we have identified and removed them as of today morning,' said DGP Argarwal.

'Do you think that you've got everyone who was involved in this ring, sir?' asked Norman.

'Mr Fitzpatrick, if there is one thing I am certain about, it is that we haven't got everyone. There are some very influential people who may be leading this ring, but we will keep investigating. It is my goal in this life to stop this treacherous activity, once and for all!' he said, booming with authority.

There was a knock on the door just then.

'Come in,' shouted DGP Argarwal.

The door opened and a policeman's head appeared.

'We have the rescued witnesses, sir. They've just arrived.'

'Send them in,' the commander ordered.

The door opened completely and Robert and Calvin walked into the room, looking extremely exhausted but without any obvious visible evidence of external traumatic injuries.

'Norman, I see you have made it. Welcome!' said Robert looking straight at his friend with a weary, but warm smile.

'I see you have too!' said Norman in a sharp voice, with a smile of relief.

'Sir, are you all right! We have been extremely concerned,' shouted Peter.

'Fine, thank you' replied his boss.

DGP Argarwal stood up from his seat, walked over to Robert and Calvin and shook their hands wholeheartedly.

'I am DGP Argarwal of the Delhi Police.'

'I know who you are. Your name has been mentioned several times by the criminals on our adventure just a while ago,' replied Robert.

'Oh, is that so?' the police chief remarked, in a friendly gesture.

'Yes, they were crapping their pants when they learnt that you were on to them,' Robert said, with a reassuring laugh.

Everyone in the room smiled, Robert's account totally depicted the character and reputation of the police chief amongst his subordinates. Pete and Norman laughed out in joy, as their boss had been returned safely, escaping torment at the hands of children abductors.

Robert thanked the police chief immensely for the great work they have done towards their rescue and shook his hands again.

'I was just doing the job I swore to perform some forty years ago,' the chief remarked. 'The man you should thanking, most of all, is Mr Khan. He knew the seriousness of the situation and also, did not want these criminals escaping justice, so he phoned me right away with the details. I am sorry you have had to have such a terrible experience in this, our wonderful land.'

'There is no doubt in my mind that this is a great country, for an innumerable number of reasons,' Robert replied.

'Pete is the car outside to take us back to the hotel?' asked the billionaire.

'Sir, I will sort that o—' Pete began, when he was interrupted midsentence by DGP Argarwal.

'Nonsense. Please, I will arrange for you all to be taken to your hotel by my men,' exclaimed the police chief.

It was difficult to decline this voluntary act of kindness, as everyone was tired, hungry and was desperately longing for some rest.

'Norm, are you tired?' asked Robert. 'I am only asking because I could smell the adrenaline on your breath. How long has it been since you have landed now — three hours?' asked Robert jokingly.

'A little tired — not from journey, mind you but from the adventures here in that short space of time,' the elderly man replied with a chuckle.

'Rubbish,' replied Robert. 'The day hasn't even properly started yet!'

'Oh dear,' replied Norman smilingly. 'Okay, let's get on with it then.'

They were taken in police vehicles, with the full complement of blue lights and blaring sirens, back to the Maharaja. It was now just after eight a.m. Robert and his colleagues disappeared into their respective suites to freshen-up. They all had expectations to capitalise on much needed rest. Robert had a shower and a light breakfast as the events of the last ten hours played over in his mind.

At nine a.m., there was a knock on his door. He went over and opened it. It was Norman.

'Norm, right on time,' he said.

'Robert, you need to get some rest, "old friend", particularly after the traumatic ordeal you have just been through,' advised Norman. 'Are you sure that you are all right?'

'Of course, I am fine, Norm,' he replied patting him on the right shoulder. 'It's whether the rest of the world is. That I am not sure about.'

'What exactly do you mean?', asked Norman. 'You are just one man, my friend. Of course, the world has many problems! But you cannot possibly save the world from all of its problems.'

'I know that, but there is one that is imperative for us to fight together,' the businessman said sternly, as looked his at his friend straight into the eyes.

Norman knew from the tone of Robert's voice and from the stare in his eyes that he was serious. They have undertaken seemingly impossible challenges before and seen them through successfully. There was now the strong feeling of another brewing in the horizon.

'Norm, we do not have all the time in the world here,' Robert began as he explained to Robert about the poor homeless boy, and the many others like him he had come across in the city. He explained to him about the impact this has had on him and the genuine need to do something to help these poor kids.

'Rob, I don't know…' began Norm. 'Is this really for you to sort out?' he asked.

'No Norm, but I can't do this on my own, even with all the money in the world. I would need your help,' said Robert passionately.

'I really don't know, my friend,' Norm replied. 'This is a massive problem that would need a huge effort to resolve. The magnitude of the effort required is best done by the authorities, who have the necessary resources to do so. We are just here to hire some bright folks. Let us do what we came here to do, and let's leave the authorities to do their work,' the lawyer pleaded.

'Norm, you have seen what is happening. No one cares a damn for these kids. They have no chance at life, no safety net, no love, no care, no nothing!' shouted Robert exasperatedly.

'They are at the mercy of the next group of villains who would try to capture and smuggle them off to paedophiles and/or used for spare parts in the dodgy underworld of illegal organ harvesting.'

'But surely, the authorities are well aware of this problem,' reiterated Norman.

'But they just ignore it, because it is more convenient to them, to do so,' Robert thundered. 'Who is to say that if these kids were given a fair chance at life, they won't be any less of a genius that any of those that we are taking away from this country to work in my company?' asked Robert.

'Rob, you are my dear friend. But why on earth would you go about sneaking around in the dark to take some food and blankets for a bunch of kids in the dead of the night?' he asked. 'You have all the resources and influence in the world. Surely there must be a better way to do this!'

'You are right, Norm. We are dear friends and there are different ways of doing this,' Robert said. 'But I do not want to create a world of artificial care and love for these kids. They won't accept it. Although I never slept on the streets, I was once an orphan, too. These kids need real love and care. Money can't provide that. Only then you will win their trust. Once you have won their trust, then will they settle down and embrace the world, and all that it has to offer them.'

'Okay then, Robert, I see. I will support you,' agreed Norm.

'I appreciate that, Norm. You are a great friend.'

Norman left Robert's suite to finish off some work before both gentlemen met again at eleven a.m. for their private meeting, which was pre-planned with Norman by the CEO before he arrived, through a phone call two nights back. Following this, Norman met with the fifteen successful candidates that Robert wanted him to meet with. He went through the special contract he had prepared for them and had them sign these for their new posts in California.

Chapter 14
Dances with a Master

A hero never gives-up

Following the meeting with Norman earlier that day, Robert did not feel as if he should continue his pursuit of seeking the welfare of the homeless kids from underneath the bridge at that point.

'I am glad to see that you have finally come to your senses,' Norman remarked. 'I was beginning to think that you needed to see a shrink,' he said, half-jokingly.

'Well, you know Norman, I do not feel as if I should abandon those kids altogether, though, because doing so would be like trying to sweep a gigantic problem under the carpet,' Robert said. 'However, I believe and accept that the authorities are better placed and equipped to deal with the problem rather than myself,' he admitted.

'Well done, my friend,' replied Norman. 'Now you go and get some rest, you workaholic devil!'

'I just might follow your instructions this time,' agreed an exhausted Robert.

'Let's catch-up for dinner, shall we?' Norman asked, 'If you are not in prison or anything like that again by then.'

Both men chuckled.

'I think that it would be a great idea,' replied the CEO. 'Maybe we should invite Mr Khan to join us; he saved my life earlier today, mind you.'

'Splendid idea,' said Norman in agreement. 'I will have all the arrangements made. See you then.'

Robert slumped onto an arm chair in his hotel suite and immediately succumbed to his compounded fatigue, accumulated over the last few days, even before Norman had completely exited the door. For him the world did not exist for several hours, as his internal machinery rebooted and reenergised. When he woke up, he used some time to catch up with some pending paper-work before deciding to go and have a walk outside, to explore the beautiful city and to take in some fresh air.

Together with a couple of his security entourage, he headed in an easterly direction for a mile before taking a side street that led to a plethora of narrow tributaries. As he proceeded further and further into the parenchyma of the city, the brio of the environment became more and more palpable in form of the collective tones of the voices, cars, machinery, activities and apparent chaos.

You cannot experience a new land without allowing your soul to mingle with those of its people. Not just any people, but the ones who silently and unrewardingly give their everything towards the life of the place. Robert was excited as he thought that he was just now starting to truly experience this interesting land.

As he walked along, his senses were bombarded by the many bright colours of the buildings, clothing and cars. The fresh odour of the street food stimulated unrestraint salivation. The infrastructure here was of a time before, when life was much simpler. The constant involuntary physical contact from fellow pedestrians on the crowded pavement, as people had no fear of each other, bred tolerance amongst them and certainly obliviated the need for the "company" Robert thought it was important to bring along. The smiles and nods of acceptance were plentiful as they perfectly complemented the noises and chaos on the streets.

The roads were crowded with small cars and bicycles of all makes. The sounds of the car engines and horns, together with the frequent chimes of the bicycle bells, created a happy and persistent musical chorus in the background of the voices of the people speaking loudly in their native language.

This background noise was suddenly drowned by the honking of a loud horn followed by the screeching of tyres. Spectators screamed loudly, as much as their lungs would allow. Then a loud thump was audible, as metal collided with bones — human bones. Robert looked across the road in shock, to visually assess the source of the sudden sense of panic.

There, across the road from where he was standing, was a young boy, wearing a dirty, tattered shirt and khaki pants, lying unconscious on the street with blood weeping from his forehead, staining the asphalt-lined road. As he rushed over as fast as he could, the space around the boy was immediately crowded by people, as curious as he was.

Robert forcefully made his way through the crowd to the unconscious body, lying face-down on the road. Despite the number of curious onlookers, Robert was the first to kneel over the boy. He carefully turned the boy's body over. He was bleeding profusely from the wound on his forehead but fortunately, was still breathing regularly, with a rapid pulse. He placed his bare hands underneath the boy's head, gently cushioning it from the coarse surface of the road and used his handkerchief to apply pressure on the wound to stem the bleeding.

He immediately ordered his bodyguards to contact an ambulance to take the boy to hospital. At this point the driver came out of his vehicle and made his way into the where the boy was lying, and screamed at the unconscious victim at the top of his voice.

'You crazy, useless kid! Why the hell did you run across the road like that!' he shouted. 'Were you trying to kill yourself?'

Robert glanced around but found no one, no responsible adult coming forward to claim responsibility for, or to provide care to the kid. By then, others in the crowd had also joined the chorus in condemning the kid for crossing the road irresponsibly. As it turned out, the boy noticed a small bag of bread that was dropped by a pedestrian and it laid on the road. He tried to retrieve it before the oncoming vehicles crushed it. He did not make it in time.

By now, with the pressure applied to the wound on the kid's forehead, the bleeding had stopped and Robert used a wet cloth to try to clean the blood off the boy's face. Tears began rolling down his cheeks when he saw that the boy was the very same homeless kid he had noticed before at the worship site and who lived under the bridge. His frail tiny body was made up of nothing more than a skeleton of bones. He was wasted and dehydrated.

As the blood loss subsided, the boy gradually regained consciousness and stared Robert straight in the eyes. He noticed the tears streaming down the foreigner's face as well as the kindness, concern and love in his eyes. The intense fear in the boy's eyes liquidated into submission. And for the first time, Robert sensed a feeling of trust from the injured boy. Laying in the arms of the stranger for the second time, protecting him from his vulnerabilities, seemed like enough to conquer this fear and protective insecurities. The boy finally appeared to succumb to trusting another human being. A great battle seemed to have been won at that moment, just there.

The people in the crowd continued to make insensitive comments in relation to the boy. Robert found it difficult to process. There was a lot of love here, but not enough for the least fortunate in the society; the ones who needed it the most; the homeless kids. It was probably a reflection of the hard life that these folks endured; so much so that they had no resources to spare, not even love.

Ten minutes had passed since the ambulance was called, yet still there was no sign of one arriving anytime soon. In desperation, Robert firmly instructed that the boy was transported to the hospital with the vehicle that hit him. The driver disagreed as he had to get back to his work. One of the bodyguards approached the driver and forcibly took the keys off him. With the help of some of the locals, they carefully placed the injured boy onto rigid board they had borrowed from a nearby vendor, and transferred him to the tray at the back of the old pick-up and drove him to a nearby hospital five minutes away. A local, who accompanied the men, provided directions to the hospital.

The medical team came out of the small hospital to attend to the patient immediately and then safely transferred him into the building. A young lady in a brown saree approached the men asking for the next of kin of the boy. Robert put himself forward and gave his details. He also signed the payment forms and waited anxiously on the corridor of the hospital while the patient was attended to.

After almost two hours had passed, an elderly doctor, in a flowing white coat and with a stethoscope draped over the back of his neck, approached Robert.

'Good evening, sir,' he said. 'How are you related to the patient — the young boy who you've brought in earlier to the hospital?' he asked.

'Good evening doctor. I happened to be passing there when the accident happened,' Robert replied.

'You are a kind gentleman,' the doctor replied.

'So, how is he? Is he going to all right?' asked the businessman.

'He sustained a mild concussion and a laceration on his forehead which has been sutured. He has a lost a bit of blood and will need a transfusion. I have arranged for this.'

'Is he going to be all right?' Robert asked.

'Yes, but we will need to admit him overnight for observations. Does he have any parents, relatives or guardian?' the doctor asked.

'As far as I am aware, no. He is an unfortunate but extremely brave kid. He is homeless,' Robert replied. 'Can I meet with a social worker to see what sort of arrangements could be made for him to be homed after discharge?' Robert asked.

'Look sir, I do not mean to sound insensitive, but there are thousands of kids like this one in this city alone. It is impossible to home them all.'

The doctor continued after a brief pause. 'I could try to see what could be done by the only social worker we have here at the hospital, but I've got to warn you that it is unlikely that she would be able to do much.'

As much as he was disappointed on hearing this, Robert understood what the doctor was trying to tell him and thanked him for his care of the little boy and for the medical attention he provided to him. This left Robert in deep thought, racking his brain for a solution to this crisis. The one thing for certain was that he could not send this boy back out into the wilderness of this city to fend for himself, all alone.

"No kid deserves this kind of neglect," he thought to himself.

Well at least, he had a whole night to come up with a solution.

It was then that he suddenly realised that he was late for his dinner appointment with Norman and Mr Khan. He phoned Norman.

'You are a no-show,' exclaimed the lawyer.

'I am sorry,' replied Robert.

'Where are you? Don't tell me that I have to come and get you out of jail for the second time today?' asked Norman half-jokingly.

'Well, you might not believe this but I am in the hospital.'

'Oh, dear Robert, are you all right?' asked his friend in a genuinely concerned manner.

'Yes, I am. I am here with one of the homeless kids who had a nasty accident on the street.'

'Is the kid going to be all right?'

'Yes, he needs to stay in overnight for observations.'

'Rob, you stay there we are coming over.'

About fifteen minutes later, Norman arrived with Mr Khan, carrying a bag in his hand. Robert was delighted to see them.

'Rob, we have brought the dinner over to you, seeing that you could not come to the dinner,' joked Norman.

'Sanjay here told me that this is the best food in all of Delhi,' Norman said, as Mr Khan shook his head approvingly.

As they laid the food over the small table in the waiting room, Sanjay identified every dish and the ingredients used in its preparation. The food was not disappointing. The three gentlemen enjoyed it thoroughly.

After dinner, Norman asked, 'Rob, so what the plan here?'

'I do not know. I honestly do not know,' he replied. 'The one thing I do know, is that there is no way that this poor kid should go back to living on the streets, after all that has happened in just the last twenty-four hours,' Rob replied.

'Rob, I have known you for a long time now. But had I not shared your experiences today and the plight of these kids, I would not have understood your passion for wanting a better life for them,' Norman declared.

'How did it go with the contracts?' asked Robert, seemingly changing the topic of conversation.

'It went well, just as you wanted," replied the lawyer.

'Norman, you do not know how much your support means to me. Thank you so much and thank you for being such a great friend and always being there for me.'

All three men sat there and had a long discussion for several hours. Sanjay Khan was extremely helpful and supportive. There was a spark that then kindled a great friendship amongst the three men after that evening.

Chapter 15
Dances with Kindness

The fire of passion is the key to success

Just after noon on the following day, Robert had a call from Calvin, who was at the hospital, keeping an eye on the boy who was an inpatient at the hospital.

'Boss, we have a situation over here,' he cried, with a sense of concern in his tone of voice.

'What is it Calvin?' enquired Robert curiously.

He was hoping to hear some sort of miraculous news, such as the boy's parents had found out about his situation, came over the see him and maybe would take him home.

'The police are here to take the child away.'

Robert's heart missed a beat on hearing this and his voice took on a more serious tone.

'What do you mean? Why have they got involved so suddenly?'

'The hospital called them as the boy was now ready for discharge and said that they could not discharge a minor who did not have a parent or guardian looking after them,' Calvin explained.

'And the police were the next logical choice then?' asked Robert, satirically.

'Fine then, Calvin. Just try to stall them until I get there. I have to make a few calls before and then I will be on my way.'

An hour later, despite the best efforts of the bodyguards to stop them, the police officers were just about to escort the child out of the hospital room. The boy sensing this, tried his best to make a run for it, but was quickly stopped by a burly officer just outside the door. He began screaming and shouting at the top of his voice as he attempted to fight off the strong hold of the officers, but to no avail. The quick and assertive response from the officers resulted in him becoming paralysed with fright.

Robert, together with Norman and Sanjay, had just arrived, and walked into the hospital room.

'Officer, please let go of the child!' instructed Robert.

'Sir, you might be a powerful billionaire, but in this country, I do not take orders from you,' responded the burly officer, easily identifying Robert.

'Officer, please put the child down!' echoed Sanjay. 'I am not a billionaire but a proud Indian! If you think that you cannot listen to my friend over here,' he said, pointing to Robert, 'then you should listen to me!'

The officer stared into the eyes of the angry retired military veteran, and released his grip on the fragile child when he noticed the fire in the eyes of the older gentleman.

Robert turned towards the lawyer and said, 'Norman, please hand these worthy gentlemen the paperwork.'

Norman, opened his brown leather briefcase and extracted a thin stack of documents which he handed over to the policeman closest to him. By then, the nurses in the room had called for the doctor in charge to handle the commotion which had developed.

Norman turned to the doctor and explained, 'Doctor, my client over here, Mr Robert Lancaster, has secured the necessary permissions from the relevant authorities to establish a home for these unfortunate kids who, through no fault of theirs, have fallen through the cracks of society.'

'It is our intention to enrol this young man into this newly established orphanage,' Robert interjected.

'Do you have the paperwork to support this, sir?' the doctor asked, looking at Robert.

'I will need your help with this, Doc, if you don't mind, please?' Robert asked obligingly, with both hands clasped and resting on his chest, which was a common and acceptable gesture of humility within the local society.

'What is the address of this institution?' asked the doctor inquisitively.

There was an anxious silence in the room as the newly formed orphanage was yet to have its location figured out.

'Block M, Near Moti Maharaja, Greater Kailash, Part Z, Delhi, 90098789,' replied Sanjay Khan, much to the relief of the other two gentlemen.

'Okay then, sir, I need to speak to the child first' replied the doctor.

He took the boy aside and asked him how he felt about going to live at an institution with other kids. He explained to the child that he would no longer have to live on the streets. He also explained that he will have all his basic needs met there until he was much older. He spoke to child in Hindi, which was the native language, as the boy did not understand a word of English. The boy firmly declined the offer.

The doctor relayed this to the gentlemen and told them that at the end of the day, he could consent for the child to go, even without the child's consent.

Robert stepped forward and spoke to the doctor.

'Allow me to speak to him, please?' Robert asked.

'Sure sir, go ahead. But he does not speak any English,' the doctor said.

'That's okay, I will translate for him,' volunteered Sanjay.

Robert walked up towards the boy, looking directly at him. For the first time, the boy did not move or attempt to run away from him. Instead, he stared back directly at Robert, in an accepting manner, and did not appear all that scared any more.

'Son, do you have a name?' asked Robert, in a kind and loving tone of voice.

'Patar,' said the boy in a soft and shy voice.

'Son, I am sorry about all of this,' Robert started, whilst kneeling down in front of the child. 'We will not hurt you in anyway. We want to look after you and try to give you a better life.'

'So, you are not one of the bad men?' asked the boy.

'No, I am not. I just want to help you. You deserve a better life. A life like any normal kid should,' Robert told him.

'Can you take me to my mother? Do you know my mother?' asked the boy, looking at the floor in sadness and avoiding eye contact as he asked.

'Where is your mom?' Robert asked, pleased at the possibility that this unfortunate kid may actually have a known living relative.

'I don't know,' replied the boy with tears rolling down his cheeks.

The next thing the little boy said tugged at the hearts of Robert and everyone else in the room.

'Instead of helping me, can you find my mom? Can you help her instead? She needs help more than I do.'

Robert was lost for words. Here was this unfortunate five-year-old kid who had nothing, who lived on the streets without care or love from anyone, and when, for the first time, he was offered help, he was willing to trade that help for the happiness of someone else.

Robert composed himself a little and replied to the child in a soft, hoarse, heart-stricken voice, 'As we do not know where your mom is, how about we look after you? I want you to grow up strong and smart, and then you can go and look for your mom. She would be happy to see how you have grown up. And then you could look after her and give her everything she needs then. How does that sound?'

The boy looked up at Robert and for the first time smiled, with a twinkle in his eyes. He clasped his hands, held them onto his chest and replied to Robert, 'Thank you, Baba,' bowing his head slightly.

Robert remained kneeling there and felt love like he had never experienced before. It was like the heat from the warm glow of a comforting fireplace melting his heart. He could not control the balls of tears, toppling over each other, down his cheeks. Tears of love; tears of a kind of satisfaction that was difficult to describe; tears that moved him immensely to a place where nothing else mattered.

Robert stood up and stepped back, while the doctor approached the little boy again, and asked him for the second time whether he would like to go to the orphanage, and this time, the boy agreed completely. The doctor signed the discharge papers and handed them to the nurse. The doctor was so moved by the kindness in the heart of the foreigner that he went up to Robert with clasped hands on his chest and bowed in reverence.

Sanjay then approached Robert.

'Okay, let's go home!'

Norman walked over to the billionaire and gave him a congratulatory pat on his back.

'Congratulations, my friend. I have admired you for a lot of things, but now I do so more than ever.'

'No, Norman, we did it together,' Robert stated, looking at Sanjay as well.

Outside the hospital, there a vehicle already waiting for the men to take them away, with the child.

'This might sound silly, but where exactly are we going?' asked Robert.

'Yes, where exactly?' echoed Norman.

'We are going to my home,' replied Sanjay. 'The boy will remain with us until the new place is available.'

Robert had already had instructed his team to look for a suitable building for the new orphanage. On the way, his cellular phone rang.

'Boss, we have found a plot of land three hundred square acres large, with a large derelict building that used to be a hospital, on the outskirts of the city. I think this would be perfect,' said Anna, one of Robert's business managers.

'Excellent. Let me know what you think after you have seen it,' replied Robert.

'It's great, I have already seen it. It needs a bit of work and the contractors think it could be ready in a month's time with a bit of a push,' said Anna.

'That's great.'

Robert turned to his friends, Norman and Sanjay and told them both the great news.

'The boy could stay with us in the meantime. My wife would be delighted to look after him,' said Sanjay.

'That's fabulous Sanjay,' replied Robert.

'Robert, do you have any immediate plans for enrolling the other kids from under the bridge to the home?' asked Norman.

Robert stopped for a moment and subsided into deep thought.

'None of these kids should spend another night, unnecessarily, in that hell hole. We should get them to safety and care, as soon as we could. I am afraid that we would lose some of them if we do not act fast,' said Robert decisively.

'We have nowhere to accommodate them for the next month or so,' pointed out Norman. 'I mean Sanjay and his family have been gracious and kind enough to accommodate Patar, but correct me if I wrong, they would not be able to accommodate a few hundred kids, surely.'

'Then we set up a temporary shelter on the compound of the new facility, so that we can carry on enrolling as many kids as we can. We need to take as many of these children off the harsh and dangerous streets as possible,' demanded Robert.

Robert got back onto his cell phone and made a few calls, giving clear instructions for the setup of a temporary shelter for the kids. He also instructed his team to begin recruiting qualified teachers and workers for the new home.

When they arrived at Sanjay's home, his wife and few other friends were already waiting outside to greet them with a bowl of freshly made jalebi and other sweets. Robert,

Norman and Patar were introduced to Sanjay's wife and friends, and they were invited in.

Sanjay's wife, Laxmi, was a retired headmistress. Sanjay updated his wife on the ambitious plans. Cognisant of the great challenge ahead, she spoke to Sanjay in private. Afterwards, they both came out to address their guests of honour.

'Robert, Laxmi and I would like to say something,' said Sanjay. 'We have just discussed this and we both admire your passion for these kids, and your dedication and commitment to this project. It is indeed a challenging one. The time has come for me to retire from my job. I pledge every minute of my time going forward to you and this project.'

'Likewise, I will as well,' said Laxmi. 'I have tremendous experience in children's education and would be happy to serve!'

'Mr and Mrs Khan, I could not thank you enough for your kind hospitality and help,' said Robert.

Both Robert and Norman were delighted. It was at that proud moment that The Lancaster Foundation was born.

Chapter 16
Dances with Change

A spark of kindness is all it takes to ignite the flames of change

There was an excitement that was unmatched within the local community, with the establishment of this special institution for the socially-displaced kids. This bred unrivalled levels of motivation which stimulated the engagement of many in the local community. The response was immense and heart-warming. The locals came forward in droves, volunteering their kind time and services to this worthy cause. It was a display of the triumph of humanity within the community. This was all facilitated by the closely knitted social and community networks within the city.

Robert was humbled by the overwhelming response of the local community towards the establishment of the Lancaster Foundation. He had come to realise how wrong he had previously been when he assumed that no one cared. He realised that here, like most other large cities, people worked so hard and devoted so much of their time to making ends meet, on a day-to-day basis, that sometimes their focus became too narrow, and they therefore missed out on the opportunities to appreciate the life that exists on the periphery of their existence. It was therefore easy for people to fail to appreciate that the life on the periphery interacts intricately with that that they pay most attention to. One inevitably influences the other. The dances of one's life was intricately intertwined with the dances of all of the others.

Robert brought in a strategic team from California to develop firm plans on the infrastructure and corporate organisation within the institute. In order to support the local volunteers, he asked the team to recruit the most suitably qualified professionals from other parts of the world to join the team. He assigned Sanjay as the Chief Operating Officer of the institute as it had become obvious to him that the gentleman, who had now become a close friend of his, shared a passion for this mission, almost equivalent to his.

Within twenty-four hours the temporary tents were erected on the grounds of the institution to accommodate the kids and all categories of staff. The area around the temporary tents were fenced off for their protection and Calvin provided five colleagues to train the locals in providing security for the kids and the team.

Against what would have been considered as an almost insurmountable challenge, the setting up of the infrastructure and team was happening just about effortlessly. It was almost miraculous. The bigger challenge laid ahead, however; fulfilling Robert's pledge to have the kids transferred to the new site. He knew that this would require a herculean effort to convince the other kids to adopt this as their new home.

Although the kids were currently living in squalor, without any support of any kind, they had found a way of achieving a type of homeostasis with their environment, as cruel as the conditions were. But they never had an opportunity to know better. Their main defence against the frequent malicious elements of society was their mental prowess, although they had never seen the doors of a school. This was supported by their sheer determination and will to survive another minute, another hour, another day and another year. This was what kept them going.

The idea of having to adapt to a more structured manner of existence would be all too radical for these kids. Both Robert and Sanjay knew that this would be the biggest challenge of all. But where there was will, there was always a way. They explored various ideas together on how they could sell this idea to the other homeless kids. They thought that it would be best to visit the arch under the bridge on evenings when the kids came there to retire for the night. They would aim to meet with them and show them the advantages of being in a home with a big family.

'These kids have faced the worst under the bridge. They sleep with "one eye open", so to speak,' Sanjay told Robert.

'They are used to be awaken during the night by paedophiles and child smugglers who are sent by their bosses to capture and bring them back for either themselves, or to be shipped abroad, never to be heard of again.'

'It seems that they are regularly harassed by the local police as well,' added Mrs Khan.

'They are not going to easily trust us or any other strangers,' surmised Robert.

In the meantime, Patar was brought into his new temporary home in a large tent. The tent had all the basic amenities for several individuals. Patar had his own bed for the first time, with clean sheets and a pillow. The things, one normally would take for granted, were unimaginable luxury for this poor kid.

There was a large kitchen, a play tent and several other tents where classes were to be held. On the grounds adjacent to the tents, was a massive playfield. Sanjay and Preethi Khan worked tireless over the previous twenty-four hours and had put together a large team of volunteers who all came with experience in childcare. The whole place was starting to pulsate with vigour and energy; of cooperation and togetherness; of love and happiness.

On that evening, Robert established a small team of volunteers to go back to the arch under the bridge to try to enrol the other kids to the home. The team included Sanjay and a few of his motivated volunteers. They brought along several hundred packed meals for the kids, knowing some of them, despite trying their very best, would not have succeeded in obtaining anything to eat for the entire day.

Upon arriving at the arch, the light from their torches triggered alarm with the kids who were already there. There were screams of panic as the kids picked up their cardboard 'mattresses' and ran for 'safety', disappearing into the darkness of a less-than-safe, modern city. Any chance that the altruists may have had at success that evening escaped into the darkness of failure. Although dismayed by their fate that evening, they placed the meals in a corner with a small lamp and left.

They all returned to the tents and formulated another plan to return the following morning. Robert returned to the Hotel Maharaja just in time to have a final dinner with his friend, Norman Fitzpatrick, before Norm set off on his journey to the airport to return to the States.

As Robert walked into the restaurant, he was escorted to the table where his guest was already seated and awaiting his arrival.

'Norman, I am sorry to be late,' said Robert to his elderly friend.

'Nonsense,' exclaimed Norman. 'Don't worry about it'.

Robert bowed his head in appreciation of his friend.

'So, tell me Robert, how did it go this evening with the kids?'

'Argh, they all ran away when they sensed us approaching.'

'Well, I can't say that this was unpredictable,' pointed out Norman. 'It would be difficult for those kids to trust any stranger.'

'Well, this is going to a major challenge for us,' said Robert.

'Have you given any thought to maybe taking the little boy along to speak to and interact with the other kids? After all, he would be able "to speak their language" on many fronts, if you see what I mean,' suggested Norman.

'Do you mean that Patar would be the best one to convince the kids that they can trust us and that we want the best for them?'

'Yes, exactly!' replied his friend. 'How is the boy anyway?' he enquired.

'He is doing well so far. At first, as you know, he was a bit reluctant to interact and was a bit quiet but he is coming around... yes, he is,' replied Robert nodding his head.

'Rob, how much longer are you planning on staying here?' Norman asked.

'Don't know the answer to that one just yet. There is something great happening here and I need to remain here as long as it takes to get things firmly off the ground…then I would return home.'

'Mind you, I imagine that I would need to return here on a regular basis. This project needs me. This is going to induce a seismic shift within this society and, by no means is it going to be an easy uphill battle,' Robert deduced.

Norman leaned over towards Robert and patted him on his shoulder.

'Rob, I want you to know that I have always admired you. But for what you have done here so far and you are continuing to do, I admire you even more so,' Norm told him.

'I could not have done this without you help and support, my friend.'

'You can rely on my unwavering support for as long as I live. You are good man and a great friend,' replied Norman.

The both gentlemen bade each other farewell as they left, with Norm entering a car and headed towards the airport and Robert making his way back to the temporary shelter. He saw no point in staying at the luxurious Maharaja Hotel any more, whilst all the volunteers were working around the clock to get the mechanisms of the institution established and functioning. He stayed, just like many others did, in a small tent on the same grounds.

Robert was awoken at four a.m. by the loud and impolite crowing of nearby roosters, although they were not easily visible. They had a well-orchestrated arrangement of sounds as they followed each other one after the other at times, and then at other times, several crowed in unison. They managed their act without a conductor and their music was most effective as an alarm for the early conquerors of the day.

Robert emerged from the tent for a walk, enjoying the cool breeze against his face. He noticed the shadow of a little person sitting outside on the ground, with his knees flexed and his legs held firmly to his chest by the embrace of his arms. As he moved closer, he recognised that the person was Patar. Unlike previous encounters, Patar looked relaxed and in deep concentration. It was the happiest that Rob had seen him. And the amazing thing to Rob, was that he did not attempt to leap up and run away, upon looking up and seeing him approach this time.

Patar looked at Rob and smiled at him.

'Hey there, Patar, good morning! You are up quite early', Rob asked

Patar paused for a moment and then replied, 'Namaste, Baba,' he said, in a shy and soft voice.

It was difficult for Rob and Patar to extend their conversation any further as they both did not understand each other's mother tongue. Rob went over and sat next to the boy, assuming a similar posture as him. They both sat there, enjoying the beauty and silence of dawn. As the sun began rising in the distant horizon, Patar pointed to the sun creeping up into vision and looked at Rob, 'Suryadeva!'

Rob repeated the word, 'Suryadeva'.

'This is called "Sunrise" in English,' he told the boy.

'Soonrise?' repeated the boy, turning over to Rob and smiling happily.

The love he felt from the kid melted Rob's heart.

By then, there was the sound of activity again, with noises of metals clanging and the symphonising voices of the individuals nearby. The others were up. The volunteers were pleasantly surprised when they saw the little boy sitting alongside the philanthropist, with his arm around the body of the boy in a warm embrace. A battle had been won. But the war ahead was evident.

As the sun was becoming more and more proud in the beautifully orange-hued skyline, Patar held on to Rob's fingers and attempted to pull him in a direction to the east. After about a hundred metres or so, they approached a painted stone idol of a god.

'Bhagavan Krishna,' said the boy to Rob.

'Okay,' said Rob, as he recognised the god as the same as the one at the altar, off the side of the main road near the bridge in the city. Robert did not know which one of the gods this reference was being to as there were many gods worshipped here. But he surrendered to the peace that he was feeling at that instant in time.

Patar gently stroked Rob's arm to steal his attention away from the god as he stood in a firmly upright posture and clasped his hands, pressing them against the front of his chest. He looked towards Robert and with his eyes, instructing him to follow suit. Robert complied without hesitation. Patar then closed his eyes tightly and began singing a beautiful and moving song in a foreign language.

Robert immediately recognised the song as the soul-touching melody he had heard before at the altar. Patar sang loudly and with an unrivalled passion. Robert felt cheated as he did not know the words to join in. He realised that he now going to have to make the effort to learn this new language.

Chapter 17
Dances with Trust

Trust is earned

At breakfast, Robert got together with some of the volunteers, in addition to Sanjay, Preethi and Patar. They all sat around a large make shift table with a mobile top, supported by two elongated pyramidal-shaped wooden structures and lined with plastic chairs outside the kitchen tent. The volunteers had come to prepare a delicious meal for Patar and the staff, as the night surrendered itself to daylight.

Robert had not had this feeling for many years, sitting around a table sharing a meal like this, but more importantly, sharing in the love of a common purpose. It was a lovely family atmosphere. As he tasted the food, the complement of flavours guided his senses to a feeling of swimming effortlessly through an ocean of happiness and joy.

Towards the end of the meal, he spoke to Sanjay.

'We need to discuss a strategy to encourage the other kids to come over.'

Preethi, who was sitting next to Sanjay, turned towards Patar to speak to him in the local language, Hindi.

'Patar, how are you this morning?' she asked the boy, who was smiling and looking at everyone around the table with affection in his eyes.

'Fine,' he replied. 'I wish that my friends were here too.'

'Do you have a lot of friends?' she asked.

'I have a lot of brothers and sisters under the bridge,' he replied. 'Sometimes, we share things like food and things.'

'Do you think they would want to come to live here with you?'

He hesitated for a bit and then a sadness crept over his face as he lowered his head, shaking it gently, from side to side. Everyone, paused in silence as they shared the sadness that this young boy was feeling. The burden felt a little bit more tolerable when shared amongst all the others.

Robert moved over to the boy and knelt down. Looking at the boy directly into his eyes.

'Son, we all want to have all of your friends here so that they too could be with you. We want to be here for them too. We are not going to leave you on your own any more; we want to look after you and your friends.'

'I know that,' he whispered softly looking down at the ground again. 'But my friends won't come.'

'They might…', Robert whispered to the little boy. 'I will go and do everything I can to get them here with you.'

'No, Baba, don't. They won't come,' he insisted. 'I can't stay either,' he whispered, as he started crying softly.'

'Why won't you stay?' asked Robert.

'I have to go back to help my friends,' he said. 'If I am not there… I have to be there to protect them,' he said, as voice changed tone.

'Protect them from what?' asked Robert.

'From the evil men that come at nights to take them away, like they did to Rishi and Sunita and Deepak…' the boy said, with sadness in his voice.

'Son, you are safe here. Everyone here is someone special who is only here to look after you. Your friends would be much safer here as well,' Robert told him.

'See that building over there, that's where you will be staying and going to school, when it is completed.'

'Wow, it is big, big, big!' said the boy, a bit more cheerful now.

'That is only one part of it,' said Robert. 'It is going to be much larger in the next few months.'

'But I have never been to school before,' mentioned Patar nervously.

'Oh, school is fun. It is where you learn about things. You could learn to be like anybody you like,' Mrs Khan said to Patar.

He looked up at the picture on the t-shirt of one of the volunteers and smiled.

'Like Amitabh Bachan?' he asked pointing at the picture.

Robert was a bit confused by this, as he did not know who the person was.

'Sir, Amitabh Bachan is a legendary movie star here in India and every child wants to be like him when they grow up,' said Krish, one of the volunteers.

Robert chuckled.

'Would you like to ask your friends to come to live with you?' asked Robert. 'We will take you to the city today.'

The boy flashed a smile as he laid his outstretched arms on the table and wiggled his body, nodding his head slightly at first but then more convincingly.

As they left the table, Sanjay approached Robert.

'This is too risky, you know that, don't you?' he asked Robert.

Robert pursed his lips and stared into empty space for a brief moment before turning to Sanjay.

'It is a chance we will have to take,' he said softly.

Robert and Sanjay, together with two volunteers, travelled with Patar in Sanjay's new SUV to the city. They parked the vehicle and walked the rest of the way with Patar, who led them, with a level of courage deficient in most adults. As they passed the tiny temple with the altar of the God, Patar stopped, approached the statue and clasped his hands firmly and bowed his head. He then proceeded along the path to the arch under the bridge.

Not surprisingly, as they got there, the emptiness they found was replaced by an unpleasant pungent odour.

'Well, it is mid-morning, I am not so sure this is the best time to come here to meet the kids,' said Robert.

'We may have to wait here for a while till the kids come by,' said Sanjay.

At that point, unexpectedly and to the shock of the men, little Patar made a run for it. He quickly disappeared into the darkness of the tunnel. Sanjay was about to go after him, when Robert grabbed hold of his hand and stopped him.

'These kids are very cunning,' he said to Robert, disappointedly.

'Hmm,' replied Robert. 'There is a saying that, "If you love a bird, then set it free! If it comes back to you, it is to be, if not, it was never meant to be",' said Robert contemplatively.

'He will come back. That boy will come,' he added.

'Please take me to the altar?' Robert pleaded.

'But what if the boy returns in the meantime?' enquired Sanjay.

'He will. But not so quickly,' Robert replied, as there was a place in his heart that trusted the young boy a lot.

The men walked calmly along the dirt path that led towards the small, make-shift tent, off the main road where the large idol of the god was sheltered. The sun was now out in its full might and it was becoming unbearable, especially for the foreigner. This however, did not deter them from the journey, although Robert's fascination with the temple bewildered them.

As they arrived, Robert noticed that the atmosphere was different from what it had been on the occasions he had previously been there. The shed was covered by a large tree which offered shade to a relatively large area surrounding the idol. It was quiet and completely exenterated of all the passionately devoted followers that he had previously noticed. It was devoid of the brotherly love of the attendees, all with the common adoration for the idol under the tiny shed.

As they approached the shed, Robert walked ahead and stood before the idol and looked around, as something was missing.

'The few times I been here, there were congregations of people chanting a song,' Robert said to the others.

'It is one absolutely beautiful song, with a melody that reaches deep down inside and touches your soul — like pure love does,' he continued in a half-distracted manner, whilst in deep thought.

'Do you know what it sounds like?' asked Sanjay.

'Jai Jagdeesh… I don't remember the words, but the melody can melt you in an instant,' he replied. 'But you know what, this is where I saw Patar for the first time and he knows the song very well. In fact, he sang it to me this morning just before dawn.'

'That is a prayer hymn that is sang to the god here. This is a murthi or idol of Lord Krishna,' explained Sanjay with other two men looking on with interest, nodding their heads.

'How come there is no one around now?' enquired Robert.

'Oh… the people only come here twice a day. First thing in the morning before work and at six p.m. after work, on their way home,' Sanjay informed him.

'Maybe Partar will come by here this evening then?' asked one of the volunteers.

'You are right… that is if he is going to return. I have my doubts about this' Sanjay pointed out.

'No, I have a strong suspicion that he will return and will do so to the site where he left us,' Robert replied in a confident tone of voice.

Sanjay and the other two men walked up before the idol and paid their obeisance to the marble carving, as Robert looked on with intense curiosity.

'Let us go to a vendor cart on the main road; I would like you to try the best food you could in Delhi,' said Sanjay, turning towards Robert and giving him a friendly pat on his back.

'Better than the breakfast we had this morning?' questioned Robert in an unbelievable tone of voice.

'The best!' replied Sanjay, smiling at the American.

After a five-minute walk along the main road, they stopped at a vending cart on the side of the road that was parked directly in the line of the moving traffic. The vendor, dressed in a cream-coloured, untucked-shirt and a weathered brown pants, stood at the front serving his customers, perplexedly unperturbed by the fact that the traffic chaos could have been alluded solely to him. The air was noisy and charged with life; a city fully awake and full of the many dancers on the stage of life. Robert enjoyed the nectar of the atmosphere, far different from anything he was accustomed to, but one that put him at ease and afforded him a barrier from the stresses of his routine day-to-day existence, especially over the last few days.

The pastry was provided with a serving of curried chickpeas along with a variety of condiments, all of various wonderful flavours and all of which had the one common characteristic of being spicy. It was a delight to him and a treat for his oral taste buds. Despite the splendid flavours and the highly delicious pastries, no fuss was made here in this wonderful world. Everyone just got on with their lives and were just happy doing so.

As he looked around hoping to maybe, catch an eye of Partar or any of the other homeless kids, he realised that it was impossible to do so in such a crowded and dynamic environment.

'Maybe we should be getting back to the arch under the bridge to see whether the boy has returned,' Robert said to his companions, with a hint of fading hope in his voice.

They made their way back to the spot where they last saw the boy, but to their utmost disappointment, he was not there and there were no signs that he or anyone else had been there since they left.

'We have got to give it time,' said Robert hopefully.

'Maybe we should split up and search areas of the city around here? suggested Sanjay.

'I will stay here in case the boy returns' stated one of the volunteers.

They all separated into two groups and left. They combed through the busy streets of the city as far as they could, in the hot and humid atmosphere, for hours. They enquired from passers-by and street vendors along the way, but no one could provide a single useful hint that would lend a ray of hope in their quest. Morale was drawing low, as hope of finding the boy rapidly faded.

At six p.m., they regrouped at the altar on the side of the main road, hoping that the boy would return there for the evening prayer, but their hopes were again left unfulfilled. They then returned to rejoin their colleague at the arch under the bridge. He was still there — all alone. There was no sign of the boy. The sun was setting and the daylight was rapidly giving up.

'Maybe we should be getting back now,' suggested Sanjay.

There was a long pause before Robert finally replied, 'No, let's give it a bit more time.'

By this this time, all the men were exhausted and starving. Patience was running low; hope was almost lost. They sat on the bare ground, leaning against the stained bricks of the wall as despair crept in. After another hour or so, Sanjay tried to convince Robert that they should leave, but he insisted on waiting a bit longer.

After fifteen minutes or so, a flickering of light became visible at the end of the tunnel, with a low rumble of noises as the darkness of the night was setting in. The brightness grew more and more intense and so did the noises from the approaching crowd. This perplexed the men and, based on their previous experience, created a sense of fear within them.

'What is happening?' asked Robert.

'Maybe we ought to run; get out of here as fast we can,' suggested one of the volunteers.

'No, hold on,' said Sanjay bravely. Robert immediately agreed.

Just a few moments later, the men noticed that there was a massive crowd approaching, with some holding flame torches on sticks. They were headed directly towards the men. But, strangely enough, as they approached, the noises died down to almost absolute silence. At that point, the men could recognise the person leading the crowd. It was Patar! He was holding on to a flame torch and followed by what seemed like hundreds of kids, of all ages.

Robert stood there speechless, amazed and cried with happiness. He knew Patar would return. He already knew that the boy was fearless, emotionally strong and honest. But what he was about to learn at that moment was that the boy was also a true leader!

He spoke in Hindi, which Sanjay kindly translated for Robert.

'Baba, I am back. I will only go back home with you if you also take all my brothers and sisters.'

'Patar, you are already a star, my son! Of course, of course, we will take everyone and we will look after you all,' replied Robert, kneeling before the boy.

Chapter 18
Dances with Victory

Without a fair chance, the talent of the most gifted would be buried forever

It was approaching ten o'clock in the evening; the sun had already retired into the night's sky. The temperature had started behaving and the constant echoes of the daily life in the nearby village had now been drowned by the creeping silence. This sense of peace was, nevertheless, challenged by the increasing sense of worry amongst the initial small staff of volunteers at the site of the institute.

'Where could Sanjay and the others be?' asked Preethi. 'They left early this morning and we have not heard a word from them since.'

'I hope they are all safe,' pitched in Amrika, one of the volunteers.

'Maybe some of you should go back to the city to find them,' suggested Mrs Khan, turning her attention to a couple of men to the left of her.

'Mrs Khan, maybe we should give them a bit more time,' said one of the men.

'No, no, no, it is much too late now,' she said. 'It is not like Sanjay to remain out this late without sending word.'

At that point, the long driveway to the site was brightly illuminated by vehicular lights, accompanied by the thunderous sounds of heavy-duty vehicles approaching. This was not what any of them expected, by any stretch of the imagination. Any ray of hope was suddenly dampened, not by fear but, by surprise and curiosity.

'What on earth is happening?' asked Preethi.

'It looks like an army of buses approaching,' replied Patel, one of the volunteers.

The buses were not of a single transport company but were covered in logos of various companies.

'It feels like an invasion of some kind,' whispered Amrika.

At that moment they noticed, for the first time, that the entourage was led by a smaller convertible SUV with Mr Khan at the wheel and Robert visibly standing on the back seat, waving his hands, providing directions and coordinating the movements of the chain of buses. There were over a hundred of them.

As the vehicles approached closer to the tents, the smile of triumph on Robert's face was undeniable. The confident driving of the military veteran conveyed an undoubtable message of excitement and victory.

Before the vehicle could make a stop, Robert hopped off and headed directly to the group, who were anxiously awaiting their arrival. They were relieved that the men were safe but, at the same time, equally curious about the entourage they had brought back with them from the city.

Robert was short of breath with excitement when he shouted at the top of voice to his colleagues at the edge of the tent.

'We have won, we have won big today!'

'What's happening?' shouted Preethi.

'Partar left us earlier this morning and spent the entire day convincing all the kids he could find to come to the site. We now have over 2000 kids who will sleep in safety tonight and every other night hereafter, who will have regular meals tonight and hereafter, and who will be given back their chance at a real life, the chance to build a future, things that they had given up on and had come to believe that they would never have a chance in this lifetime to have or to experience! This is going to change from tonight!' said Robert, almost gasping to catch his breath.

'Patar is a truly remarkable boy!' cried Robert, with tears of joy flowing freely down his cheeks.

'Srini, please take everyone. Go to the houses and shops here in the nearby villages and out in the city and collect all the food you could as soon as you can,' ordered Mrs Khan. 'These kids are going to very hungry. We need to feed them.'

'Please go,' echoed Robert. 'Tell those kind people that they will be reimbursed tomorrow for any food they could spare us tonight.'

'This has caught us by surprised,' said Patel, as he approached Robert. 'Sir, we are not equipped at all to accommodate these kids, not today night, not even for a while. The facilities are just being constructed, we don't even have enough tents for these kids to sleep tonight. Would it not had been better to wait for a month or two before bringing the kids here?'

'I would not even entertain the thought of even one of these children spending another night in a such an unsafe place in the city,' replied Robert firmly.

'But sir, you say this, but look what is happening here. Do you think that they are any better here?' Patel asked.

Robert stood in disbelief on hearing this, especially considering the passion he had of ensuring the safety of these kids. It became obvious to him that Patel did not quite understand the severity of the problem; the deprivation these kids experienced, or the danger they faced every second of their lives on the street.

'Patel, dear friend, maybe you are right that tonight we are not fully prepared, but come tomorrow we will be in a better place. The most important thing though, is that tonight, each of these kids is much safer,' said Robert reassuringly.

'How could you say that, you do not know that for sure,' argued Patel.

'Under my responsibility, these kids are going to be safe tonight and every other night hereafter,' replied Robert sternly.

'You are not Indian, you cannot understand Indians; how do you know about what these kids are like?' Patel asked Robert argumentatively, raising his voice at him.

'Enough!' ordered Mrs Khan to the gentleman. He was obviously looking to pick a fight with the businessman.

Robert could not help but turn to the man.

'You do not have to be anything else but human to recognise the plight of these unfortunate human beings.'

Robert thought that the current situation demanded his urgent attention far more than an argument with this gentleman.

'Excuse me,' Robert said, as he turned and walked away. He went immediately to phone his friend, Norman, for advice. He described the situation to him and the urgency of the problem. Norman was already thousands of miles away. He reassured his boss and asked him to leave the matter to him and he will try to sort it out.

Norman, through a contact of his, managed to phone the Governor of Delhi and explained the situation to him. The Governor was most sympathetic to the cause and pledged his immediate support. Within an hour, the military descended onto the site and began erecting huge tents to provide immediate temporary shelter for the kids and staff.

In the meantime, Srini had returned with a number of volunteers from the nearby villages, bringing with them hundreds of cooked meals and other items of food stock to last for several days. The food was taken to the kids, who were still on the buses. They were exhausted and starved. They accepted the meals with trust. Despite being stuck on the buses for almost two hours by this time, they remained calm and accepting.

The tranquillity of the night was replaced by a frenzy of activity, the likes of which, had never before been witnessed in that part of the country. Volunteers, friends, family, lay-persons, civilians and servicemen all working alongside each other, under bright artificial lights in an effort that witnessed a most powerful display of the human spirit; all ignited by the spark of one man's burning passion. One of desperate compassion for a crippling problem, never before recognised in this way, as it laid hidden in plain sight.

Within an hour of the Army arriving, all the tents were erected and fitted with basic amenities. It was a truly amazing feat. The military then left once this was completed. Before leaving, Robert whole-hearted thanked them for their immense effort. Arrangements were then put into place to take the kids off the bus and into to bed, so that they could get some rest before a new chapter of their lives started the following day.

The volunteers went through bus after bus, taking a record of the names of the children. There were many other details needed but not necessarily that late at night. Only about two-thirds of the kids were able to respond to the request. A significant number of them were not even aware of their names.

To not be aware of one's name is like having no physical existence or expectations from a world vibrating at odds with that individual. There was no index point in existence or reality for them. It robbed them of a sense of self pride. Their confidence was replaced by vulnerability in an unimaginable scale. Vulnerabilities were laid bare and left exposed to exploitation in its every form from ill-intentioned elements within the city. Survival depended solely on the possession of a strong spirit. Only the strongest survived.

The kids without names were asked if there were any names they preferred. Some had preferences, but for others, survival was the only preference they wished to entertain. These children were assigned temporary names for identification purposes. They were all given a card with their name written on it. None of them knew what the scribbles on the card meant, as they were not familiar with any writing and could not as yet read.

The kids were taken to tents and shown to their beds. The beds were makeshift, consisting of a mattress on the floor with a sheet to cover with. From the gleam in the eyes of many that night, they were delighted beyond description. For these kids, despite the simple arrangements that night, knew that they were going to have the best night's sleep that they have ever had in their entire lives.

During the course of the night, activities at the site did not stop for a single moment as there were many arrangements that needed to be taken care of. Sanjay and Preethi went home and made numerous calls to all of their acquaintances to try to recruit as many volunteers as possible for the following day and the rest of the month or so, until professionals could be hired to look after the kids.

Robert, also retired to his tent, where he insisted in living under similar circumstances like the kids and volunteers. He had a tiny wooden table which he used as a desk and a plastic chair as a seat. A far cry from his elegantly furnished office in California or his suite at the Maharaja. Next to the table was a mattress lying on the ground where he had slept comfortably the night before.

Robert phoned through to his operational manager on the West Coast to scramble a recruitment team to secure the services of the best teachers and educational professionals internationally. Everything had to happen at lightning pace. There was no room for delay or complacency. There was only a small window of opportunity to exploit, if these kids were going to remain off the streets in a safe and caring environment.

The next day, there were scores of volunteers turning up at six in the morning to the site. They were of all age groups and from across all strata of the society. Interviews consisted of a simple handshake and a smile; work-badges were 'stick-on' paper labels across their chests. The qualifications for hire included previous experience at any job, no matter what they were, and uniforms were non-existent but politeness, smiles and happiness were aplenty.

Immediately upon arriving, Preethi assumed the role of team leader and assigned the volunteers to various groups. The group assigned to food and catering immediately settled down to business in the large tent that was the makeshift kitchen, as they had many hungry kids to feed. The sun seemed to have been awoken by the strong and delicious aroma from the kitchen, transmitting beautiful warm golden rays of illumination to the site. The aroma also did the trick on the kids as well. After breakfast, they were sent to a large tent to get showered and they were given clean sets of clothes and sandals. Small groups of children were assigned to individual volunteer educators later that morning.

During the course of the day, the kids gathered on the open field. Patar was the one of the shortest and smallest of them, so he sat at the very front. After a few minutes the kids got a bit restless and began protesting in low voices. Patar stood up and climbed up on the podium at the front and encouraged the kids to have patience, and reassured them at everything was now going to be good for them.

Robert was introduced to the group by Mrs Preethi Khan and addressed them in English, which was not a language which they comprehended, but Preethi performed admirably translating throughout.

'Good morning, everyone. This country is steeped in its rich culture and its values. Although I am not an Indian, these are quite similar to the culture and values system I was brought up in. We have a high regard for our friends, neighbours and guests. The comfort of a guest is regarded as far more important than that of the host. Today, you all are our guests.

From now henceforth, we promise to look after you, to try to replace what you have been denied of so far in life: care, love, friendship, education and most importantly, hope. Hope for a better life. Hope for a safer life and hope to able to dream; to dream like any other kid anywhere else on this planet.'

'Finally, I would like to say a special thank you to the hundreds of volunteers who dropped everything in their lives to join us here today. To you my fellow friends, I would like to say what a wonderful privilege it is going to be to work with you, so that together we can serve the needs of these special little people,' he finished off, to loud applause by all.

Chapter 19
Dances with Grief

In the eye of the storm of tragedy, often lies dormant collateral beauty; you have only to open your eyes to bring it to life

The first week was a bit like a roller-coaster ride for everyone. There was so much that needed putting into place. This was punctuated by episodes of maladjustment by some of the kids to the new environment. The local volunteers were great, beyond description, at handling the emotional challenges of the children at adjusting to their new environment. They constantly worked hard to reassure the kids that they were in a much safer and better environment. There were a lot of opportunities for learning for everyone, including the ones with experience in children education. For Robert, this was all a new world, but he knew it would all come together, as it was steered by the strong will from the bottom of his heart. Nevertheless, he discovered the magnitude of the challenge. Even setting up a home for a single kid is challenging and requires immense preparation. However, in this situation, it was a couple thousand who had already somewhat adapted to a completely different lifestyle and were now being encouraged into a more structured way of life. The challenges were numerous as well as enormous.

By the end of the first week, the signs of adaptation were beginning to reveal themselves. The rudimentary or almost non-existent policies of the home were refined into more structured and useful practices. The kids began enjoying the environment and interacting with each other a lot more. Their bubbles of existence were noticeably coalescing into a common one by a force of attraction fuelled by hope and humanness.

The construction company had been working non-stop in an attempt to get the premises ready as quickly as they possibly could. Robert met with the lead engineer, who confirmed to him that the facilities would be all ready for moving into in amazingly, one month.

"What an achievement that would be!" thought Robert to himself.

Robert received another set of great news that day. He had a call from the HR folks in California to inform him that they had successfully managed to recruit just over two hundred professionals to teach and look after the affairs of the institute. They were recruited from a number of well-recognised institutions internationally, and they all were in a position to start within one month, at the latest. All the bits of the puzzle were finally falling into place. Robert and the team were jubilant.

Robert held twice-daily briefings with all the volunteers, due to the highly dynamic situation of the project, in order to update them of new developments. At these briefings, he also sought feedback from the staff on how the kids were coping and whether any strategies needed to be tweaked. That evening, he addressed the team.

'Good evening, everyone. Namaste, my friends. I am pleased to inform you that we have now successfully recruited professional educators and educational support staff, like some of you here today. They will be here in a month's time. The other good news is that the building we will be permanently occupying across the field will also be ready in a month'.

Everyone applauded at the great news.

'It is indeed an honour to work with every one of you. I would prefer if every one of you stayed with us. But if you have to leave us at the end of this month to get back to your regular work, please know how much I have appreciated your help in setting up this project and for all the love and care you have shown towards to these kids. Finally, although we will miss you, we would never forget you', said Robert.

After a long day, once all the kids were in their respective beds and everyone had retired for the day, Robert went out for a walk along the long driveway that led to and from the site. As he escaped the brightness of the lamps at the site and walked further into the darkness, the night's sky became more and more beautiful, as it was strewn with its inter-galactic sparks. The air was fresh with the aroma of floral perfume. He felt a kind of peace creeping up on him; a kind of peace that had eluded him for much of his lifetime.

As he walked into the moment of tranquillity, he reminisced on a life of perpetual challenges and the efforts needed to overcome these. He thought about the love and the opportunity he has had to sacrifice to experience this. It was surreal, yet magical. He also dared to remember the bitter side of love and losing it. He looked back on the times he spent with Margot, and yearned deeply for one more moment with her. He would exchange anything for a chance like that.

After losing her parents, Margot developed a sense of guilt that was extremely difficult to shake off. This inevitably posed a significant mental strain on her. In fact, even for someone who was as emotionally strong as she was, this burden was far too much for her to shoulder on her own. She bottled it up and stifled her feelings as life gradually became more and more a pretence. This had a significant impact on her emotionally and mentally. She suffered immensely — in silence. Robert had since often kicked himself for not recognising it. But to be fair, she was good at hiding it from, not only from him, but to the world around her as well.

Following the monumental disagreement that the couple had, resulting in an intense fight, Robert was deeply perturbed by her irrational and erratic outburst that evening. He was too deeply hurt to have recognised that this was the one and only time that the burden of her stress physically manifested itself. He regretted it each and every time he thought about it ever since.

The following morning after their fight, he went off to the office, too upset to even kiss her goodbye, something he did each morning. Later that morning, he sat over a cup of coffee and regretted fighting with her. He was going through emotional turmoil that day himself at a deep and personal level. This left him vulnerable and incited an emotional upheaval in himself.

He wrote a note to her and sent it with a bouquet of beautiful red roses.

My Dear Margot,

I am terribly sorry for upsetting you last night. I have never seen you that upset before and I apologise profusely for putting you in such a position. We have always promised not to keep secrets from each other and I want to honour this promise.

There is a lot about my life which I have never talked about. I barely remember my parents. They were killed in a tragic accident when I was an infant. They dropped me off to school that morning but never made it back to pick me up. They were not only devoted parents but wonderful people as well — I remember, vaguely, someone telling me.

I lived in an orphanage for the best part of my childhood, with the perpetual expectation that one day they would still come to pick me up. But then I grew wise enough to understand that that would not happen and that I had to move on. I longed so much to spend even as much as one more day with them.

I understand that you are a principled person and I support you wholly. I cannot thank you enough for standing up to your parents and supporting me in the way you have, but they are your parents and it would make me happy to see you unite with them, even though they may not like me.

Yesterday was a hard day for me emotionally. I was adopted by a couple when I was eleven or twelve years of age. I moved across the country and was finding it difficult to adjust to my new world, my new life. They were unable to cope with my issues and they opted to end the adoption.

This couple visited me in my office yesterday to apologise for their decision to give up on me. It was too emotional charged for me to handle. I came home a bit upset. I fought with you to subconsciously to relieve myself but I ended up upsetting you. Sorry. All I needed was a hug. I am sorry for my awful reaction.

I love you more than anything else in the world, more than life itself. We will get through this and anything else that life throws at us, together.

Love Always,

Yours,

Rob

Robert knew for certain that she read it, but regrettably, neither of them had a chance to discuss it. Sadly, later that day, Robert received a call from the hospital that Margot was admitted in a critical state after she attempted to commit suicide. Every cell in his body froze in shock, despair and regret. He immediately left in a panic to the hospital but by the time he got there, it was too late. She had passed away only moments before.

When he was given the news by the senior doctors, he fell unconscious onto the floor, sustaining a laceration on his scalp which bled tremendously. The tremendous sorrow that he felt was released through the steady and heavy flow of blood from his wound. Not even tears could have accomplished this more effectively. When he regained consciousness, he hoped that the last few moments that he recollected were all part of a cruel dream. He then found out that there was no one there any more to comfort him. After a while, he composed himself, sat upright and thought to himself that he had been through too much in his incredible life to forget the painful lessons he had had to learn throughout. He knew that he had to be strong; he had to be strong for Margot's sake and his. Able to understand the reasons that brought her to do this. He still loved her more than anything else in the world and he still strongly believed that she loved him as well. The pain, compounded by the guilt that this attracted, was potentially preventable had he not had that nasty fight with her the night before. It was unbearable.

It was at Margot's funeral that he came to find out about the source of her tremendous stress. Margot decided to visit her parents to make amends a few months earlier, thinking that now they would be willing to accept Robert as the love of her life. When she got there, the front door was locked shut and the huge glass windows were boarded up. There were no signs of life there. The lawn had not been mowed in ages and the plants had obviously not attended to for a long time. A sign on the front door read, 'No Entry'.

She drove away and stopped off at the nearby town for a coffee. When she enquired from the barista about the people who lived in the country house just outside the town, she asked Margot who she was.

'I am Margot, I used to live there with my parents,' she replied.

'Do you not know?' the barista asked.

'Know what?' she asked in an apprehensive voice.

'They died a few months ago. They both committed suicide.'

The cup of coffee she was holding in her hand fell to the floor as she stood there and stared blankly into space, in shock and regret.

'I am sorry, so very sorry,' she apologised, as she bent over to pick up the cup.

'No worries, we'll get this cleaned up,' said the girl behind the counter.

Margot walked away quietly back into the car, bent over the steering and wept until she was short of breath. She never mentioned anything to anyone, including Robert. But this was a weight far too heavy, even for strongest to carry. It was the most emotional of crises to have to face. Alone.

At the funeral, Robert was left there feeling cheated for not being able to be with the love of life again, to tease her, to laugh with her, to grow old together. He was angry that she, who meant the most to him, was taken away so cruelly. He just could not reconcile with her loss.

Oscar had since blamed his dad for his mom's death and hardly spent any time him. He only called his dad once in a while. The forces keeping them apart were more overwhelming than Robert had wished.

Robert had since remained unsettled emotionally. However, ever since he had initiated this project to house and rehabilitate the underprivileged kids, his heart started mending. It was never planned to be like this, but this was what felt right to him. He was just following his heart again. It had taken him many years to reach this stage. But never a day went by that he did not think of Margot and what their lives could have been like had things been different.

He made his way back to the site and was walking towards his tent, when he noticed one of the kids sitting on a pile of bricks, staring into the night. As he approached closer, he recognised that it was Patar.

'Patar, what are doing out here so late? You should be in bed, shouldn't you?' asked Robert.

Patar looked up at him and smiled.

'Going… bed sir. Waiting for you come back,' the little boy said, as he tried to speak in English.

Robert accompanied Patar to his bed and tucked him in. He then returned to his tent and settled down to bed. As he laid in bed, a smile swept across his face, thinking what a gentle heart that little kid had. He was out there, waiting for him to come back before he could go to sleep. He was touched by the gesture.

It had now been two weeks since Robert had been in India, and the pressures from his work in California were mounting. He needed to get back to the States for a few days to sort out urgent business before returning. He knew that he could not stay away from the site for more than a few days, as the whole project was still very much in a fragile state.

Chapter 20
Dances of Two Worlds

Nothing could survive an existence in isolation

Robert entered the boardroom at the company's headquarters in Los Angeles to find a roomful of black suited men and women, all with disposal cups filled with millions of drops of liquid black magic. They needed this desperately, to get through the morning at least. They looked up at him with sharp and intense eyes. It was business. He assumed his usual position at the head of the table and opened the meeting.

In his absence over the couple of weeks, there were a lot of reports to catch up on. Robert was delighted that business was excelling and congratulated the board members. He took the opportunity to give a briefing on the philanthropic work that he was engaged with in India. This was, generally, well-received. He requested the board to consider supporting the efforts of the newly-formed charity, 'The Lancaster Foundation for the Improvement of Life'.

There was unanimous support for this from the members and Robert then proceeded to direct the CFO to formalise arrangements for the funding of the charity.

'Sir, don't you agree that we need to formalise a budget for this?' asked Timothy Hoffman, the CFO.

'Yes, get it sorted then,' replied Robert sharply.

Mr Hoffman, a medium-built, bald gentleman with bushy eyebrows, raised his hand in the air again.

'Go ahead, Tim,' instructed Robert.

'What I mean is that shouldn't we, as the board, agree upon a spending limit for this charity?' he said, as he looked around the room for support from his colleagues. His eyes did not find those of anyone else in the room. They all wanted to distance themselves from the Hoffman's line of inquiry, as they saw this philanthropic cause of the CEO as a worthy one.

'I do not see that that is necessary, my dear friend,' said Robert. 'This is one of the most financially successful companies in the world. Its success will not only be judged by its financial wealth, but also by how much it contributes to the uplifting of the world and bettering the lives of the most unfortunate.'

There was silence in the room as everyone nodded in agreement, except Hoffman.

'Sir, with all due respect, and this is not, in any way intended to diminish the importance of the work you are doing, but would it not be fair to think that this money could be better spent to improve the lives of regular, everyday Americans?' asked Hoffman.

'Mr Hoffman, I do not disagree that there are poor kids here in America, but the magnitude of the problem there in India is enormous, beyond acceptable.'

'Do you think by helping a few kids or a few hundred kids or even a few thousand kids, would resolve a problem like this and of the magnitude that you have alluded to?' questioned the CFO.

'After all of this, even if just one kid has a better chance at life, it would be worth it.'

Robert then ended the meeting. He spent a busy couple of days catching up with his work and had the opportunity to catch up with Norman. He took delight in relaying the sequence events that happened after he had left and the success which they have had at the end.

He did manage to catch up with the human resources team, who were working extremely hard to recruit the professionals for the institute in India. He browsed through the profiles of the various educational professions including teachers, sports facilitators, musicians and paediatric psychologists.

'This faculty is indeed very impressive,' he told the staff.

After three days in California, Robert flew back to Delhi to help with the preparations in moving into the new facility. The volunteers were extremely happy for his swift return. Robert held meetings with each of the administrative and operational teams to finalise policies for the start of the 'Lancaster Institute'.

One week prior to the grand opening of the institute, the international professionals began arriving. They were provided with comfortable accommodation in a separate building of the compound. They were all very keen and brimming with excitement. The educators then had the opportunity to meet with the kids and to start building a rapport with them.

The kids were initially quite reserved and scared, as they were not used to interacting with many adults before and, even more so, foreign adults. English was the chosen language that was taught at the institute, and even in the matter of a few weeks, their vocabulary was coming on dramatically well.

The day finally arrived and, without the pomp and ceremony that it deserved, the large campus was opened. Work continued straight away. A ginormous task laid ahead and everyone recognised the importance of getting a head-start. All processes were put into place for the smooth and safe running of the institute. The classrooms were all equipped, together with the built-in gyms and music rooms and a mini-concert hall. There were meticulously-crafted governance measures integrated into the system to safeguard the kids and staff. Support structures and processes were also put into place. It truly was one of the best educational facilities in all of Delhi, at the time.

Robert, as chairman of the institute, carefully scrutinised the running of every aspect of the institute and implemented tools to track the progress of the students. He spent part of the day in the office and the other times, he actively embedded himself into various parts of the system to help out and assess its functionality. It gave him a chance to identify problems that others may have missed and the chance to liaise with the appropriate folks to resolve these.

He worked harder than he had ever worked before in his life, but enjoyed it even more than he had ever done before. As time passed by, he had settled into a routine of spending one week per month in California and the rest of his time at the institute in India. The initial chaos of a hastily developed facility — like this was — gradually improved as the months passed by. By then, Robert found that he had more free time in the evenings, which he enjoyed spending with the kids, playing a game called cricket.

Cricket was the most popular sport in India and was a common mutual love amongst everyone — the old and young, rich and poor, talented and not so talented and the educated and uneducated. Every boy dreamt of being a professional cricketer. Although the ball used in professional games were dangerously hard, this was often substituted for by soft tennis balls when the game was played for fun by amateurs. A bowler, batsman and wickets-keeper were complemented by a number of fieldsmen who would spread out throughout the field to hamper the chances of the batsmen scoring a 'four' or 'six'.

In addition to being a naturally talented batsman, Patar had a natural leadership talent and this was most evident on the field. He was able to encourage his team mates to become better players and was great at setting admirably high professional standards. Although Robert was crap at the sport, he often admired the natural talents of the young kids.

On evenings after dinner, Robert would often join other teachers, who took turns at reading for small groups of kids before they settled down to bed. The kids had grown fond of his kind, gentle and supportive nature. He became popularly known as 'Baba' amongst them. This was a name given to him by Patar. After everyone had gone to bed, Robert often found the time to rekindle his interest in music and began learning to play the cello. Often, he would take his instrument out far away from the lights of the buildings, where he would settle down in a quiet corner to practice strumming the strings of the wooden box.

As he became more confident in playing the instrument over time, he often tried playing the ancient hymn he had heard many a time before, the melody of which had haunted him ever since he heard it for the first time at the altar, off the side of the main road, in the city centre. He experimented with many different variations of notes to perfect even further, a tune already perfected, over many millennia. The joy this brought him every time was indescribable. While playing, tears would flow down his cheeks as the music massaged his soul to create moments of oneness with an absolute truth.

In many ways, he needed these moments to himself. They gave him strength to face the great many challenges he constantly faced on a daily basis, and invigorated his determination and confidence to survive in a world which could be cruelly turbulent in all sort of different ways. The lives and survival of so many others directly and indirectly depended on him.

His visits back at his workplace in California became more and more difficult, as he was finding it more and more challenging to cope. Leading the business became more daunting to him. This was a direct result of the waning support of his colleagues and board members, apart from a few loyal friends, such as Norman. After a year, the board voted to cease all contributions to the institution. Robert was extremely upset about this but pledged his continued support for the institute, by directly funding it with his own money.

He instructed Norman to arrange the liquidation of some of his assets, which included his impressive LA mansion, in order to continue funding the institute.

'Are you certain you want to do this?' asked Norman.

'Norm, you know what the stakes are, if I don't?' Robert asked him rhetorically.

'I know how passionate you about this,' Norman replied.

'I have no need for all this money and luxuries now, Norm. Besides, there is enough to fund Oscar and his educational needs,' said Robert.

'How is Oscar, by the way?' asked Norm. 'Do you two talk regularly?'

Robert paused for a while, looking down at the floor. He then slowly raised his head and looked up into space before replying.

'You know what it is like. He still hasn't forgiven me for it,' as he pursed his lips.

'Do you reach out to him?'

'I try... well, I used to try much harder before, but nowadays I have to accept that our relationship is probably never going to be all that great ever again. But we still speak briefly from time to time.'

With his hands in pockets and pacing slowly in front of his boss, Norman looked him in the eyes.

'The question needs to be asked, and please forgive me for this, Rob,' he began, 'do you suppose that your passion for the kids in India is some kind of psychological substitute for the fact that you can't fulfil an inner desire to be closer to Oscar?'

Robert looked him squarely in the eyes and replied immediately in a firm tone of voice.

'Norman, that is wrong! How could you think that? It is about those kids being homeless, family-less, love-less and needful in every way imaginable. They have no safety net at all!'

'Rob, you know that I know that and I fully support you, but being your friend, I just needed to ask.'

'Thank you, Norm, you are great friend indeed,' said Robert patting him on the shoulder.

Robert returned to Delhi soon afterwards and continued managing and supporting the operations of the institute in every way he could. The success of this effort was rapidly becoming obvious even to the disbelievers amongst them, such as folks like Patel. The kids were flourishing academically and in various extracurricular areas. They were all fluent in English, and other foreign languages such as Spanish, German and French. Some were extraordinarily talented in music, such as Partar.

Word spread far and wide throughout Delhi, about the educational prowess of this institute. This prompted the newly-elected Governor to send a written request for students from privileged backgrounds to attend the school as well. Robert declined this, as it was against the founding principles of the school. The institute was not established to become an academic facility, but rather to improve the lives of the less fortunate homeless kids. Even if the kids were not academically-inclined, this was viewed as equally acceptable. Once the needs of the children were taken care of and they felt safe, then the institute would have achieved its objective. If the kids excelled academically, then that was a bonus. Those were the founding principles of the institute.

Chapter 21
Dances with Desire

The nectar of sacrifice feeds love, hope and survival

As the years passed by, the institution grew stronger. The staff became more and more adjusted to their unique situation and adapted well, despite the many challenges. As expected, there were a few for whom the conditions were either not right, or the challenges were too much for what they were willing to offer, so they left, but those posts were quickly replaced with more passionate teachers and other educational providers from various corners of the world.

The kids who were once accustomed to wearing torn and dirty clothing were now connoisseurs in fashion styles. Whereas in their previous lives, survival was the challenge, now they were exposed to a number of mind-blowing subject areas and extracurricular activities to explore — a different challenge. The options were not only multitudinous, but quite varied and catered for the various interests of most, and not of any single group of individuals. Interestingly, the difference with this group of children was that there was no need to teach them about the value of life. They stumbled onto this a long time before they came there.

The kids were always encouraged to pursue fields that they not only enjoyed, but demonstrated a passion for. They valued the simple things in life such as caring for one another and not wasting opportunities. At the institution, they were taught the values of simple everyday manners and respect for themselves and for others.

Although they received a well-balanced general education in the basics, they all had different special interests and great attention was taken by the staff to help each and every one of the kids nurture and develop their special interests and talents. Witnessing their progress was like a special privilege for everyone, especially Robert.

Within the institution, there was a great emphasis on discipline. At some stage in their late teenage years, they were going to have to go out there and face the world again. It was Robert's mission to ensure that this time, they would be most prepared and ready to interact and conquer the world. A world that could be awfully cruel to the unprepared, and could swallow up the less disciplined.

Robert was appointed as a teacher as well. He went around from class to class, giving lessons on life. He called that subject 'Ethics'. He enjoyed doing so a lot, but the students loved his classes even more. No one ever missed "Baba's" classes. To the students, he was like an uncle providing them with advice that would see them through to a wonderful life.

At the age of ten, Robert noticed that Patar was a bit distracted and was not able to concentrate during class-time. Prior to this, Patar was an exemplary student — a straight A student. He also was elected as the leader of the debate group, as well as the editor of the junior student magazine. He was a very bright boy. So, naturally, this change bothered Robert somewhat. Despite, casually approaching the boy on a number of occasions over many months, Patar insisted that all was fine. Robert did not bring up his faltering grades, but tried to find out if there was a problem at all and what it was, if there was one. The sheer will and determination this young man had was usually enough to repel problems of any sort — well, usually.

One evening, Robert went for a walk in the playing field after nine p.m., once the kids were in their beds. He searched for a quiet, dimly-lit spot to self-isolate himself for a bit. It was the personal time he afforded himself to spend in isolation, to extract himself from the on-goings of everyday life. He did this a few times per week. With him, he carried a foldable chair and his cello strapped across his right shoulder. He set his chair down, removed the cello from its case and set it up. He had by now become a master of playing that ancient Indian hymn. The melody usually reached down to his soul and massaged it. Every time, playing that particular tune would bring tears to his eyes.

As he started to play, he closed his eyes tightly and savoured every note. His muscles relaxed throughout his body as his consciousness ignited. His protected space was suddenly interrupted by the noise of rustling behind the bushes nearby to him. He wasn't sure who or what it was. He stopped. He looked around and then placed his cello against the chair as he walked towards the bushes. As he approached the bushes, someone came out, with his head bent and walked towards him. It was Patar.

'Patar, what on earth are you doing here?' he questioned. 'Shouldn't you be in bed by now?'

'I am sorry Baba, I just wanted to hear you play that beautiful song.'

'What's it called?' asked Robert, feeling a bit foolish that he did not know the name of the piece.

'Jai Jagdeesh Shahare,' replied Patar.

For those who knew Patar, he was always upbeat, full of energy and wore a permanent friendly smile across his lips. But there was something obviously very different about him recently.

'Patar, where has that lovely smile of yours disappeared to?' asked Robert.

Patar did his best to feign a smile, but not enough to fool the clever Robert. He stood there and looked the boy directly in his eyes, remaining silent for more than an uncomfortable moment. The boy bent his head over, but did not say another word.

Robert walked over to him, held his hand, and brought him over to the chair.

'Patar, I would like you to sit on this chair.'

The boy, still silent and with his head bent, moved over to the chair and seated himself.

Robert moved over to the side and knelt down. He began playing the beautiful tune for the boy. Patar closed his eyes and allowed the music to flow into him, displacing the tears from his eyes that had been building up for a long time. Robert noticed the tears tumbling down the cheeks of the boy, but continued playing until the very end. He then stood up and walked over to Patar, knelt down and hugged him.

'Son, are you sure that you are okay?'

Patar began to snivel as he hugged Robert tightly.

'Baba, can you please help me to find my mother?' he begged.

'Son, do have any idea where she lives or work... anything at all?'

'No,' he said whimpering. 'But she is somewhere, I know it.'

'Do you remember the last time that you saw her?' Robert asked.

'No, only vaguely. She made dinner for me and we went to bed. She went out to work. That night, a massive machine came and tore our house down. It made a loud, horrible noise.'

'Oh dear,' whispered Robert. 'What did you do?'

'My elder sister asked me to promise her that I would run away as fast as I can and to go as far from there as I could. My other brothers and sisters were still in the house when the crane began smashing it to pieces.'

'Do you know where this was?' asked a now tearful Robert.

'I don't remember. One of the men ran after me, yelling, and wanted to capture me. I ran as fast as I could and ended up at the train station. I ran into the first train that was leaving the platform and hid in a box in one of the carriages.'

'Do you have any idea where it was that you took the train?'

'No, I don't remember much.'

Robert sighed as he tried to comfort the boy. 'We will try, but it is not going to be easy. It is more likely to be impossible. But we will try,' said Rob reassuringly.

'I just want to know that she is all right and I want her to know that I am good. I want to hug her again,' the boy pleaded.

'That's okay, son. We will do our best. Now let's get you back to bed. You have a long day ahead tomorrow, I am sure.'

Patar looked up at the man he called 'Baba' and gave him a warm smile.

The following day, Robert summoned the social workers at the institute for a meeting. He informed the team of Patar's request.

'Each of our kids have had a dark experience that has led them onto the streets. It may be difficult for some of them to have to revisit these, but maybe we ought to explore the possibility of tracing their parents. It won't be an easy task but...'

'Are we planning on returning them to their parents then?' asked one of the workers.

'No, but we should attempt to trace them and let the kids know about them. They could then be a bit more reassured. This is still the best place for them, if they decide to stay.'

'These kids belong to their parents!' shouted a voice at the back of the room. It was Patel's.

'They may not have the means to support them,' said Robert.

'But they owe a lot to their parents, who may need the support of their children now,' said Patel. 'I do not know how much you know about the culture of this land, but it is the responsibility of children to look after the parents when they get older.'

'These children do not have the means to do so. But when they do, then they may wish to consider this,' replied Robert, to the anger of the gentleman.

As weeks and months passed by, despite a thorough attempt, there were no credible leads to locate Patar's mom. However, the immense and widespread effort did result in locating the parents of some of the kids. There was a similarity in these stories to Patar's. The parents were extremely poor and despite working as hard as they possibly could, it was difficult to provide care or even the basic needs for their kid.

For one reason or the other, these kids succumbed to a nasty and dark fate that eventually resulted in them fending for themselves on the streets of a cruel world.

Robert met up with Patar one morning before classes started.

'Son, I am afraid I don't have very good news for you', he started. 'We have done everything we possibly can, but in the end, we have been unable to locate your mom or siblings. I am really very sorry,' he said.

Patar smiled at him and gave a tight hug.

'Baba, thank you so much for trying so hard. I feel happy that you have tried and I hope she is fine.'

'Son, if she is anything like you, I am certain she is fine,' Robert told the boy. 'You were born into a family with whom you have spent a wonderful time with, and now you have another much bigger family to look after you. How lucky are you?'

Patar smiled and nodded his head in agreement.

Although this exercise was not successful in Patar's case or the majority of the kids at the institute, they were able to locate and meet the parent of one of the kids, Seema. Robert with other members of the team managed to contact the mother of the ten-year-old girl and visited her.

She lived in a house which was no more than a sheltered, rusted, galvanised, barricaded room, located in small area of a crowded village buried somewhere in the fringes, beyond where civilisation, as we would have imagined, ended. Contrary to what Robert expected, that which was deficient in the material wealth of the family was generously made up for in the love that the mom had for her family.

She was a single mom, as her husband died a few years from the complications of a killer, which was no stranger to the folks there — diabetes. The family was so poor that they could not afford simple medications, basic healthcare or even food on many days. She worked long hours in the fields about ten miles away from her home, travelling back and forth on foot. She had only a pair of rubber slippers that were worn thin, and hardly able to afford any protection to her feet as she made her daily journeys.

When Robert and the team visited, the mom was not at home, as she was at work. She had eight kids at home. They were looked after by the eldest, who was one year older than Seema. They waited all day for her. When she returned, she was initially scared to see "city people" in her home. She feared the worse, as interaction with people beyond the boundaries of the village was virtually non-existent.

They introduced themselves and she enquired why they were there. Robert told her the great news that her daughter was at the institute. She started crying. The reflections that bounced off the tears as it tumbled down her cheeks were that of the raw and uncensored essence of life itself — a liquified potion of intermixed joy and sorrow. The experience of a lifetime summarised in a single brief moment of time.

The mother was overjoyed to find that her daughter, who she missed so dearly and for whom she prayed daily, was safe and alive. This was balanced by the guilt of not being able to care for her as she should have. A point of equilibrium was difficult to establish. The visitors offered to arrange for her to meet Seema and to re-establish contact, and to rekindle their bond.

At the end of their visit, the lady and the kids all sat on the floor for their dinner. The mom gave them each a piece of flat homemade bread, called roti, and a cup of warm cow's milk, fortified with her love. She sat there and smiled as she watched them eat happily. She then offered Robert a drink — a glass of milk as there was no more bread left. Robert politely refused as he knew that if he accepted this kind gesture, the poor lady would have had to go bed hungry after a long day or hard work.

The following day, Robert sat at his desk in his office and contemplated on his experience on the previous day. He tried to contact the local social services but was unable to do so. Although the world could not possibly be completely homogenous, how much better would it be if it was that little more homogenous, he thought to himself.

Later that morning, a surprise awaited Robert when one of the local volunteers entered into his office.

'Sir, there is a Swami outside, asking for an audience with yourself'

'A what?' asked Robert inquisitively.

'A Swami is one of the high-standing holy men, sir,' he responded.

'Why?' asked Robert, with a cheeky smile across his lips. 'I am far from holy, and we are not even a religious institute.'

'He said would like to drop-in to have a word before he continued on his journey.'

This message perplexed the American, but he agreed to meet with him, though he did not know what he could possibly discuss with this holy man. But what he did not know was this conversation was going to send a shock wave through the fabric of his being.

Chapter 22
Dances with a Mystic

As we do not have all the faculties to understand everything there is to understand, sometimes, we just have to place our trust in fate

Despite the best efforts of Robert to exist simultaneously in his two worlds, which were virtually on directly opposite sides of the planet, issues were developing in LA. Without his physical presence and direct control in LA, it became impossible to oversee all the operations and wield his influence on the major decision making on a daily basis. Although he was easily reachable by phone and communication was not a major problem, his lack of presence in LA left a void. As is known, nature does not like voids. The laws of the universe dictate that voids are filled, one way or the other.

At board meetings, an autonomous faction was gradually developing. This was initiated and led by Mr Hoffman, who saw an opportunity, fuelled by the absence of the strong figurehead at the helm of the organisation. Mr Hoffman used his influence to gradually coerce other colleagues in order to gain their support for his agenda. He used every manoeuvre available to him in executing this, including promises of promotions, salary hikes, special favours and extortion.

Despite initial reluctance, they slowly caved into his ideology and demands. Anarchy was setting in.

'Is the boss going to join us today?' asked Mr Hoffman, at the start of the board meeting.

'No, he is in India. I have had extensive discussions with him over the last few weeks with regards to the plans we are proposing at the meeting today,' said Cathy Polinsky, the Chief Operating Officer.

'He does not seem to be around much any longer, does he?' countered Mr Hoffman.

'He can run things from there and I think that he is doing a great job so far. But I am sure it must be hard for him,' Cathy pointed out.

'Nonsense!' shouted Hoffman. 'He has chosen to abandon this ship, his responsibilities and his colleagues to gallivant in a poor, under-developed country, pretending to be the Lord of the Land. And, the worst part of it all, is that he is using our money, this company's money to do so!'

'Mr Lancaster is the head of this board and is still in command here', shouted Norman, standing up from his seat to scold the gentleman. 'Sit down, Mr Hoffman!'

'Mr Fitzpatrick, your close friendship with the CEO is a matter of a significant and noted conflict of interest,' thundered Mr Hoffman. 'I propose to this board that this is a serious matter and that Mr Fitzpatrick be replaced with immediate effect! The work of this board is paramount to the operations and survival of this company. Please indicate by show of hands,' said Hoffman in a raised, harsh tone of voice.

The board voted for Norman's replacement sixteen to fifteen. Norman immediately gathered his papers, stood up slowly, looked around the table, then bowed his head and left the room. He went to his office and attempted to contact Robert to inform him of the mood in the boardroom that night, but was unable to do so.

After Norman left, Hoffman stood up and addressed his colleagues in the boardroom again, in a further attempt to gain further support in 'filling the void' of Robert's absence. A once quiet and subordinated accountant was now invigorated with the temptation of opportunity which was dangling before him. Betrayal was a small and insignificant price to pay for this.

Meanwhile, back in India, things could not have been better for Robert or the institute. The kids were coming on at lightning speed. To survive on the streets, in the manner in which they did, required immense inner strength and determination. These qualities were not lacking in these kids at all. In fact, on the contrary, these qualities were the ingredients for their success so far, indeed. The project was so successful that, it kept expanding, constantly removing more and more kids from a life on the streets.

Robert was approached by one of the members of staff about a visiting holy man, who had called in on his long journey and made a specific request to see him. He was a bit confused about the request initially, but agreed to meet the sage in his office that morning.

When the door opened, an elderly gentleman stood at the doorway, garbed in a thick red-orange coloured robe. Robert was convinced that he was wrapped in this single piece of cloth. The man was unusually tall with long, plaited hair, mostly greyed. He boasted a long grey beard that was effective in hiding his face or any facial expressions. His skin was dark but shiny, and his fingers long and slender. The had a long stick in his right hand, which he held on to firmly.

Robert was at first confused about his attire. Although his robe consisted of a single piece of cloth, it was unusually thick. The weather in that part of the country was hot and humid, completely inappropriate for this type of clothing material. The other observation that Robert made, that also struck him as odd, was that despite this gentleman just coming straight from the streets into the building, there was not a single drop of sweat on him. Although Robert was in an air-conditioned room, he still had beads of sweat rolling down his cheeks.

'Pranam, sir,' said the holy man as he stood at the doorway, clasping his hands as he addressed Robert.

'Good morning!' replied Robert. 'Please come in and have a seat.' Robert beckoned him in and directed him to the chair in front of his desk.

The man slowly walked forwards into the office and approached the chair. To Robert's surprise, he then proceeded to move the chair aside and sat on the bare floor, with his spine upright and his legs folded. Robert did not quite know how to respond politely to this, or what he should do next. He thought that the best thing for him to do, in order not to insult his guest, was for him to take a seat on the floor opposite his guest. It dawned upon him then, that despite the length of time he had already spent in this country, there were still a lot of customs and traditions he was yet to become familiar with.

'Sir, I am Robert Lancaster, nice to meet you,' he said, as he attempted to stretch his right arm out towards the sage.

The man did not reciprocate. In a soft and confident tone of voice, the swami said, 'I know who are, I know everything about you, more than you even know about yourself.'

Robert was confused about his statement but decided to hear him out. He knew that in India, these holy men were well respected and worshipped. The last thing he wanted to do was to do something that would anger the locals.

'I want to meet you privately, please' he requested, as Robert beckoned to his staff to leave and to close the door behind them.

'Great,' said the swami.

'Who are you?' asked Robert. 'Thank you for stopping by on your journey.'

'I am Swami Pitaji. I live in a cave in a remote area at the foot of the Himalaya mountains,' he replied.

'Nice to meet you,' said Robert. 'That is a long way from here. What are you doing here? What can I do for you?'

'All you can do for me, sir, is to listen carefully to what I have to tell you. What you choose to do with it then would be all up to you,' he said, with a wavering motion of his right hand while rocking his head side to side.

'Okay then, let me hear what you have to tell me,' Robert said, in a semi-joking way.

'I have a message for you about someone in your past, who still loves you very much,' he started.

'Who is it?' asked Robert.

'Your wife,' he said, and Robert sat up sharply.

'She would like you to know that she is very sorry about how she left you, but is very proud of you for what you are doing. You should not stop under any circumstances.'

'Okay great, is that it?' asked Robert.

'Yes, it is,' said the swami.

'Okay then. Well, it was nice meeting you and I wish you all the best for the rest of your journey and hope you get to where you are going safely. I have a lot to do right now,' said Robert, a bit impatiently.

The old man remained sitting there, motionless, showing no intention to stand up to leave.

'My journey ended when I got here a few moments ago,' the swami said, after several moments.

'I thought you were just dropping in whilst on your journey. That's what they told me,' Robert said. 'What is it that you want from me?'

The man looked up at Robert and said, 'I need you to believe me. I have walked for hundreds of miles to get here to give you that message. You must believe me!' insisted the swami.

'Okay then, tell me one thing — why should I believe you or anything you have said?' asked Robert, raising his voice in frustration. 'My wife died years ago; how could she give you a message to give to me? She had never ever been to this part of world in her entire life.'

Robert's phone on the desk rang. He did not answer it. His cellular phone began ringing.

'Excuse me for a second,' he said, as he picked up his phone and declined the call.

'Did you not want to take that call from your friend, Norman Fitzpatrick?' asked the swami.

Robert was shocked. How could he have known that it was Norman on the line? He definitely could not see the caller ID on the phone. Robert took a deep breath and then told the man that that was strange but nevertheless, he was still not convinced of the tricks he was playing.

'What can I do to convince you?' the old man asked, in a low, soft tone of voice.

'Tell me something that nobody else in the world knows but me,' Robert replied.

'The day Margot died you sent her a letter,' the swami said.

He then closed his eyes and recited the contents of the letter, word for word. Robert sat there, paralysed with shock. It was like he was hit by a thunderbolt.

"Could it be that the letter got leaked on the internet?" he thought to himself.

'Tell me something else,' Robert demanded. 'Something else that no one would know.'

'The first time you saw Margot, you were at a concert hall. She wore a long, elegant, bright-red dress...' said the man, as he continued describing every little detail to Robert about how he felt towards Margot.

Robert had switched off and melted away into a surreal sea of stupefaction by then.

'I now believe you. I am sorry that I doubted you in the first place,' Robert apologised to the sage.

'You are a great man with an extraordinary soul,' the old man said softly, looking at Robert with warmth in his eyes. 'You are changing the destiny of many here. You are giving them much more than they ever would dare to dream for and most importantly, preventing much of the hardships and suffering that was written in their fate.

'Thank you,' said Robert, with tears rolling down his cheeks.

'Can you speak to Margot? How is she? Can she ever forgive me for not being there for her when she needed me the most?' he asked in rapid succession.

'She is fine, she is an extraordinary soul like yourself, hence the attraction between you both', the swami told him.

'She admires the work you are doing. She wants you to carry on doing your best to complete it.

'Soul mates are never far apart from each other,' the swami reminded him.

'Give her my best, please, if you would,' Robert pleaded.

The swami stood up, looked at Robert and asked him to walk him to the door. As they both walked together, he turned to Robert and said, 'Son, it is not going to be easy, but keep courageous, keep strong and keep up your spirit. You will have the privilege to hear her play the violin again one day.'

'How could that be possible?' asked a bewildered Robert.

'Have faith, my son. Nothing is impossible.'

As the swami was about to exit through the door, he turned around for the final time and spoke to Robert.

'In the meantime, you will have some help when you need it the most. Keep your ears and heart open and you will know.'

This last bit was too much for Robert to process at the time.

'Where are you going now?' asked Robert.

'Back to my home. My mission is now finished; I now have to return to my place.'

'Please stay and have a meal with us, and get some rest before embarking on your long journey,' asked Robert.

'Thank you, but I must get a head start' he said, clasping his hands and saying, 'Pranam.'

Back in LA, the board was still meeting without Robert, and now, without Norman. Hoffman presented the board with evidence that Robert was arrested in India as a paedophile and he was released through 'legal technicalities' with the help of Norman Fitzpatrick. Hoffman informed the members that it was quite possible that the funds transferred from the company to the charitable organisation in India, The Lancaster Foundation, was being used inappropriately for establishing and maintaining a paedophile organisation. He asked for this discussion to not be minuted and to be kept confidential.

Chapter 23
Dances with an Angel

It is important to realise that we all share a common purpose

Robert was left speechless after speaking to Norman on the phone. He settled back on his chair in his office in resentment and disappointment at what had happened in the boardroom. He knew that Norman was not well liked amongst the other members because he could be opinionated and would tell it as it is, unperturbed by what the consequences were. But the actions of Hoffman were a bit off-centred, he thought.

Robert then arranged to return to Los Angeles and he called an extraordinary meeting of the board members. Everyone was informed at short notice. Prior to the meeting, he was approached by Hoffman.

'Sir, great to see you again,' he said. 'I am happy that you have called this meeting. I detect a bit of resentment amongst the members of the board.'

'Resentment? Resentment about what?' Robert asked angrily as he paced about his office, while Hoffman stood stationary in one spot.

'Please sir, don't shoot the messenger?' pleaded Hoffman.

Robert stormed out of his office, straight into the boardroom. There, all the members were already present. He took his seat and perused some documents placed before him while Hoffman took his seat. When everyone was there, he finally looked up, stood upright and started pacing around the table slowly.

'Thank you all for attending at such short notice', he began. 'I understand that a decision was taken to replace Mr Fitzpatrick as the Head of Legal Affairs at the last sitting of this board. Would someone be so kind to explain this to me?' he demanded.

Hoffman looked at Mr Kim on the opposite side of the table and covertly signalled him to speak.

'Sir, as you know, the members of this board were made to feel quite intimidated by the gentleman in question. We, as a group, feel that this board would function better by a member who is more approachable and easier to work with.'

As Mr Kim took his seat, Hoffman signalled to another of his associates to speak. Mrs Perceival stood up and asked to raise a motion of 'no confidence' in the CEO.

'Sir, we, the board, would like to raise a motion of "no confidence" in yourself, as the functions of this board are severely hampered by your almost complete absence and lack of engagement. We have raised this motion today, as we believe that it would be in the best interest of this organisation. In addition to this, I would like to propose that Mr Hoffman should take the helm of running this company.'

The motion was seconded by Mr Kim, then another and another. It was not long after that Robert realised that this was a coup.

Robert turned to Hoffman, 'Did you know anything about this?'

'No sir, I had no idea but I do believe that the views of the members should be respected, however.'

Robert became silent. He felt deceived. He stood up and paced around the table contemplatively. The room went silent, as all eyes were focussed on him, anxiously anticipating a response.

'Do you know where the trees that provided the wood from which this table was made came from?' he asked the board members in a calm voice.

There was absolute silence.

'Do you know where the carpet that your feet are resting on right now, came from?

'I started this company. I built this company from scratch. I chose every piece of décor and furniture in this room myself!' he shouted. 'What gives anyone of you the right, to think for one moment, that you could dispose of me like an item of trash? I built this company,' he cried passionately.

'If this company means so much to you, why then are you not here running it, like you should be?' demanded one of the members.

'I damn well run it. Whether I am physically here or not. Nothing of any significance happens here without my consent,' replied Robert angrily.

'Tell us then about your criminal record in India,' asked Mr Kim, all of a sudden.

'That was all a grave misunderstanding!' pleaded Robert. 'We are doing great work there and are on our way to improving the lives of thousands of kids, who would not have a future of any kind, otherwise.'

Robert managed to regain control of the board by the slimmest of majorities after the vote was passed. He settled back on his chair after everyone had left. He was exhausted. This was a wake-up call for him and a sure sign that things were likely to get difficult, going forwards. The coup failed but the momentum against him was increasing. The war had just started. He no longer had the support of his ally, Norman, on the board.

Hoffman passed by his office afterwards to see him.

'Sir, I am sorry about the actions of my colleagues at the meeting. You know that I would always support you,' he said disingenuously.

Robert looked at him with an expressionless face.

'Hmm', Robert replied staring directly at him. He was not someone to be fooled easily.

'You know what, I would quite like the opportunity to visit your institute in India?' Hoffman asked.

'I did not know that you had any interest in the work we do over there.'

'Of course, I have always been a firm supporter of your work across there, Sir. You know that.'

'Sure, anytime. Let me know and I could help with the arrangements,' said Robert.

'How long are here for this time, before you go back?' asked Hoffman.

'Seven days.'

Later on the next day, Robert had a message from Sanjay that one of his colleagues from LA was there to have a look around.

'He is very inquisitive and has been speaking to everyone he could. In particular, he has been spending a significant amount of time with Mr Patel,' Sanjay told Robert. 'Why did you not let us that he was coming?'

'Show him a good time and let him see the great work that is happening there,' instructed Robert.

That evening, Robert met with Norman for dinner at his house. Norman was a widower, who lived in a fairly comfortable and large house in Beverley Hills. Although the house did not have a modern interior decoration, it was well laid out, neat and inviting. Norman spent the evening preparing dinner for both of them. Although, the food was wonderful, his choice of wine for the evening was most incredible. Robert savoured the moment. They talked a lot as they reminisced about the years gone by and shared a lot of laughter.

'Robert, I would like to let you know that I have been doing some thinking and have decided to retire completely,' said Norm.

'Sorry but what are you going to do with the rest of your life?' he asked. 'You won't survive for a minute without the shenanigans of the office.'

They both laughed but Norman was serious.

'Well then, come to India and help me?' asked Robert.

'Nah, too old for that now, my friend.'

'Then help me from here. You could work from home,' Robert said smilingly.

'On a more serious note, however, Robert, my friend, I am getting an uneasy feeling about the company. But I just cannot put my finger on it.'

'I can handle it, don't worry,' said Robert reassuringly.

Robert left after dinner and returned to the hotel he was staying in downtown LA. He phoned Sanjay to get an update on the institute before retiring to bed that night. Sanjay told him that everything was going well.

The following morning, he went down to the restaurant for breakfast. As he was about to retrieve two boiled eggs from the pot on the table, he accidently bumped into in a young lady. She looked about in her early thirties, pretty, blonde, neatly dressed with high-heel shoes.

'I am very sorry,' he apologised.

'Don't be,' she replied, in an attractive Latin American accent. 'No bodyguards today, I see.'

Robert was taken aback by her comment. Had he met her somewhere before? How did she know so much about his lifestyle, he pondered?

'No, they get to have some time off… sometimes. Besides there is no danger in here,' he replied jokingly.

'Well, you just never know,' she said equally jokingly.

'Sorry, I am Robert Lancast…' said Robert, stretching out his right arm towards her. She stopped him midsentence.

'Yes, I know who you are,' she said, almost flirtingly. 'I am Anna-Maria Santiago.'

'Where you from, Anna-Maria?' asked Robert, noting the beautiful accent that she sported.

'You, make a guess, why not?'

'Ahhh, don't know, but let's go with… Buenos Aires?' said Robert confidently.

'Hmm, close… but not quite right,' she replied teasingly. 'New York City!'

'Hmm, very close?' asked Robert laughingly.

'Well… New York City via Montevideo,' she teasingly admitted.

'There you go, I was close… after all!' said Robert.

Before he could ask any further questions, like how she knew who he was, she turned around and walked away with her breakfast in her hands. Although Robert felt the urge to follow her, he did not think that it was appropriate. He went over to his table and began perusing the daily newspaper, while he cracked the shell of each of his eggs with twenty-one light strikes, to the tune of 'Jingle Bells', using the back of a teaspoon. This had been his morning routine for as long as he could remember. He was about to devour the boiled eggs when he heard a familiar feminine voice behind him.

'Hello again.'

It was the beautiful young lady he had met moments before.

'You again?' asked Robert in a mirthful manner.

She smiled beautifully.

'Still no bodyguards, huh?'

'What can I do for you?' asked Robert jokingly.

'I am actually interested in your work in India,' she replied sharply.

'I am into…' she started before he interrupted her.

'I know who are and what you do,' he said, to the surprise of the young lady. 'From Harvard, to Wallstreet and now the United Nations.'

'I am impressed,' she admitted. 'You are good.'

'No, not as good as you think. But this thing is, the internet is great!' said Robert.

'So, what makes you interested in my work in India?' Robert asked.

'Well, we do have similar interests. My work is all about protecting and improving the lives of vulnerable children all over the world. I have been following your work. What you have achieved so far is impressive,' she said. 'I am back here in a month's time; can we meet up for a chat about this — over coffee maybe?'

'Sure, I would like that?' replied Robert. 'This is the number for my secretary. Have yours liaise with mine to firm up the details?'

'Don't worry, I already have her details,' she said, flashing a mischievous smile.

'I should have known,' Robert said laughingly. 'But please also take this number. It is a close friend of mine who knows everything about our work in India. You could catch up with him as well, if for any reason, I did not get a chance to meet with you next month.'

As she left, she turned around and jokingly remarked, 'You really ought to do something about your bodyguards.'

'Clearly, so,' remarked Robert smilingly.

Chapter 24
Dances with a Monster

In life, we have to be prepared to engage with the good,
bad… and the ugly

It was a glorious morning, with rays of energetic sunlight eagerly seeping through the curtain-free large windows of Robert's office at the Lancaster Institute in Delhi. It encouraged a sense of calm and happiness. Robert sat at his desk, pondering about his life. Although the road getting there has been terribly bumpy at times, it was all worth it. Despite everything, he felt a sense of achievement and fulfilment. His life made sense to him at that moment in time. His life had a purpose. He was making a difference and his dreams and efforts were having an impact in a complex world.

There, sitting on his desk that morning, was an envelope with special decorations on it indicating that it had come from an important source. It had the special stamp of the Governor's Office on it. He opened it and began reading the letter from the newly appointed office holder. He found the contents a bit peculiar.

The Governor firstly congratulated Robert on establishing such a fine institute with such high educational standards. He then went on to mention his wish for the resources of the institute to be used for the benefit of the wider population of

Delhi and should not be 'wasted' on kids that were removed from the streets. He asked that Robert lend serious consideration to his wishes.

This angered the American businessman. It was wrong on so many different levels. It represented everything that Robert despised and had worked so hard to overcome. He wasn't going to have any of it. He rang the Governor's Office and arranged an appointment to discuss the matter face to face.

A few days later, he managed to meet with the newly appointed politician, who was renowned for being corrupt. He was a short man with a noticeably protuberant tummy, thick moustache and bushy eyebrows. Robert approached him with clasped hands. The man did not even bother to reciprocate. His mannerism lacked respect. He simply signalled to his guest to have a seat with a hand gesture. Up to this point, he consistently avoided eye contact with Robert.

'What is it you would like to speak to me about?' he enquired from his guest.

'Your Excellency, thank you for taking the time to meet...' Robert started, when the Governor interrupted him.

'Please, say what it is you are here to say, I don't have much time to waste,' he warned Robert, in a low, hurried and harsh tone of voice.

'Your Excellency, it is about the letter that you sent me,' Robert restarted. 'I am afraid that I do not fully understand what it is that you wish.'

'Do you understand English, Mr Lancaster?' he asked rudely.

'Yes, sir I do.'

'Good, then it is self-explanatory, I hope,' the governor told Robert.

'Well, with all due respect, Your Excellency, that is not something I could accept and certainly it is not something I am willing to consider,' said Robert, politely but firmly.

'Don't you think that the high standards of education at your institute would better serve the needs of the more intelligent kids within our society than those from the streets?' he asked Robert. 'Don't be a fool Mr Lancaster, would you prefer to pour water on a real plant with the potential to grow… or on a plastic plant?'

'Sir, it is obvious that we are significantly different views on how we value human life,' said Robert curtly, with a flushed face.

'Do you know what karma is, Mr Lancaster?' the man asked rhetorically.

Robert stayed silent.

'Do not feel pity for those kids. Their struggles in this life are all a reflection of the bad deeds they have committed in their previous lives. If they had good karma, they would have been born into a higher caste. They have to repay for their sins they have committed in their previous lives, in this life,' his host lectured him.

'Hmm,' said Robert. 'It's not that simple, is it?'

The Governor looked at him, quite cross as he realised that Robert did not agree with his cruel stance.

'Good souls should to be rewarded, Mr Lancaster. Your resources need to be redistributed. This is what I am saying. I am not the judge here, karma is.'

'Your Excellency, with all due respect, I do not agree with your argument. Those kids are some of the most vulnerable human beings. Where is your sense of kindness, compassion and love?' Robert asked, in a raised stern and raised voice.

'Karma takes care of everything, Mr Lancaster,' the Governor responded. 'I will give you one week to reconsider your position.'

'Or what?' Robert asked.

'You will find out. I have to end this meeting now as I have more important things to attend to, as you would imagine,' said the man tersely.

That meeting disgusted Robert in an unimaginable way. The lack of compassion, care and love was incredible, especially for a policy maker of a large city where the majority of the population needed it. But by using this gentleman's proposed strategy whereby resources are prioritised for the affluent, the rest would be side-lined into a vicious cycle of poverty and lack of opportunities. Not only was his logic and philosophy flawed, he was cold-blooded and devoid of the basic sense of love for his fellow men. It was worrying that such a man was afforded the right to govern against the very people who democratically elected him.

Later that day, Robert received a call from his dear old friend, Norman.

'Robert, how are you?'

'Hmm, life is a war, Norm. You know that don't you?' Robert said half-jokingly.

Robert related the events of earlier that day to Norman who became very concerned.

'What are going to tell him in a week's time?' Norman asked.

'Go to hell, Mr Governor,' replied Robert laughingly, in order to try to make a serious issue more palatable, in an attempt to preserve his sanity.

'Well, I had a call from a young lady in New York, who I am due to meet up with in New York tomorrow,' Norman mentioned. 'She told me that you asked for her to meet me. Who is she?'

'Well, all I know is she is beautiful, educated at Harvard, worked in Wall Street and now works for the United Nations,' he responded.

'Still doesn't answer my question, Rob. Why am I meeting her?' asked the lawyer.

'She is interested in the Foundation and the work we are doing here.'

'Why have you asked for her to meet myself, and not you?' asked Norman.

'Use your imagination, Norm. You will figure it out,' responded Robert.

They both exchanged a bit of friendly banter for a short while, afterwards, before there a light-knock on Robert's door.

'Come in.'

The door opened and Patel poked his head in. Robert was not expecting him.

'Patel, do we have a meeting in the diary?' Robert asked curiously.

'No, boss. I was just checking as I heard some noise in here.'

Robert went on with his regular activities for the rest of the day.

Two days later, Robert entered into his office at seven a.m. like he regularly did. But to his surprise, the office had been ransacked. It looked as if a bomb had exploded in there. There was paper strewn across his desk, chair and the floor, in stark contrast to the manner in which he had left the place the night before. The lamp on the corner of his desk was on the floor and in pieces. He went over to the document cabinets and they were all forced opened and empty!

He immediately called Sanjay who advised him to alert the police before informing any staff members. Sanjay made it over as soon as he possibly could have and got there moments before the police arrived. He sought to reassure an increasingly worried Robert. By then, the police were on the scene.

'Hello, I am Inspector Prem,' said the head officer in a khaki uniform and several stripes on his shoulder. Sanjay emerged from the behind and the police officer recognised him immediately. It turned out that they both knew each other and with the twitch of an eye, Sanjay pleaded to the officer to carry on with his investigation. The police spent most of the morning there and left without much to offer the now worried philanthropist.

Robert invited Sanjay for a walk on the fields around the institute afterwards, while the staff tidied up. As they got to a safe distance, Robert confided in the gentleman.

'Look here, Sanjay, I am worried,' said Robert.

'Are you sure you are not overreacting?' asked his friend.

'Well, I had a rather hostile meeting with the newly-appointed Governor a couple days ago. He requested that we take in the sons and daughters of the elite at the institute and discharge our current students. He did not have any compassion or interest in our work.'

'Hmm, that is worrying, my friend. I understand your concerns. I can tell you that he is an evil man. He is very corrupt and ruthless,' mentioned Sanjay.

'He has given me a deadline, which expires in five days to arrive at a decision favourable to him,' he said, 'but I am not going to — dead or alive.'

'That gentleman does not play by the rules. He plays nasty!' Sanjay warned his friend about the new Governor.

'Can you promise me something?' asked Robert.

'This mission is my life. Under no circumstances must we fail those kids. If anything was to happen to me, please contact my other good friend, Norman. He will know what to do,' instructed Robert.

They both returned to the office, where they were told that the files of the kids and all the operational documents were missing!

'This is serious!' said Sanjay to Robert.

Sanjay took up a piece of scrap paper from the desk and scribbled a few words on it and gave it Robert.

The note read, 'We cannot speak in here. It is likely that the room and your phones are all bugged.'

He immediately became disquieted about the fact that he had no secure manner to communicate with Norman. But he sported a brave face and explained to the staff that it was all right, and this was probably a petty theft carried out by disgruntled, unemployed amateurs from the village nearby.

In the next few days, he made it his mission to meet with each of the students of the institute and chatted with them, had a laugh with them and let them know that everything was going to be fine.

Chapter 25
Dances with Scandal

With truth on your side, fear is powerless

Robert was rudely awoken by loud banging on his bedroom's door. He then heard the screaming of kids. As he glanced over towards the window, he noticed that the night sky was painted red and blue by flashing lights. He was hoping that this was just a terrible dream. Soon afterwards, his door was forcibly opened, dragging him into full consciousness. Armed officers in military gear entered the room, with scary looking weapons.

'Here he is,' one officer said loudly.

'Get him!' ordered a thunderous voice from the hallway.

'What on earth is going on here?' asked the American, just as he was accosted on the bed by the burly armed officers and muffled with a hand roughly placed over his mouth. He struggled to breathe and tried violently to release himself from their grasp, but to no avail. A black sack made from thick cloth was placed over his head and he was forcibly handcuffed and savagely escorted out of the building into the back of a lorry. It was pitch-dark. There, he was greeted by someone, the voice of which was only too familiar to him. It was the low-pitched, firm toned voice of the Governor.

'Allow me to do you a favour,' he said, as he reached out and removed the sack covering Robert's head. 'Don't say that

I have never done anything nice for you,' said the Governor, laughing mockingly.

'I am an American citizen,' said Robert with a weak voice.

'Yes, I know,' the man said.

After a moment of silence, the Governor spoke to him.

'All of this was probably avoidable, you know. Now you have to pay the consequences for your obstinacy,' he said in a harsh tone.

'Pay for what?' Robert asked angrily.

'You know,' said the man, as he left the truck.

The screaming of the kids was so loud that not even the sirens were able to drown their screams of fear. There were all sorts of other noises and commotion. Robert feared the worse. In the midst of it all, the vehicle started driving at a hurried pace. Robert was thrown backwards, bumping his head on the wall of the vehicle, and temporarily lost consciousness.

When he regained his senses, he pinched himself, with the hope that he was still dreaming. After a further half an hour or so, the vehicle came to a halt. There were noises of hurried activities outside. Before long, the door of the truck was slammed open. Robert was initially blinded by the bright rays of sunlight shining into the enclosed cabin of the vehicle. Several officers rushed towards him in an aggressive manner and moved him out into the building though a narrow backdoor. He was taken to a room where he had mugshots taken, and then was escorted into a prison cell. As he entered the room, they switched off the lights revealing a deep homogenous darkness, almost revealing a reflection of how he felt inside.

'Why am here?' Robert shouted.

There was no answer.

He sat on the cold floor of the room for several hours before he heard the noises of incoming footsteps. Suddenly, the cell went bright again. The loud clanging of the metal bolts and doors were perceptibly louder than anticipated, as two officers came in, held on to his arms and escorted himself back into a vehicle.

'Where are you taking me?' Robert demanded to know.

There was no response. He asked over and over again, until there was darkness once more, as the doors of the vehicle shut tightly. After a short journey the vehicle stopped and he was escorted into a building through a set of double doors. The officers pushed open the doors, violently dragging him in. He recognised the room. It was a full-to-capacity courtroom, filled with angry people and lined by men with large cameras.

He was escorted to towards the Magistrate's desk, where he was held firmly by officers on both sides. The judge looked up after several moments of silence and glared at him with piercing eyes.

'Mr Lancaster, tell me, how do you plead to the charge of obstructing the work of officers of the city of Delhi?' he asked.

'I would like to have my attorney present here, Your Honour.'

'I will ask you again, Mr Lancaster. How do you plead to the charge of obstructing the work of officers of the city of Delhi?'

'I would like to have my attorney,' Robert demanded.

'Foreigners accused of serious charges are not entitled to an attorney at this stage. I will ask you for the final time; how do you plead to the charge of obstructing the work of officers of the city of Delhi?'

'Not guilty, Your Honour.'

'Mr Lancaster, how do you plead with regards to the charge of resisting arrest?' the judge asked.

'Not guilty, Your Honour.

'And finally, Mr Lancaster, how do your plead with regards to the charge of sexual molestation of a minor?' the judge asked.

Robert was taken aback by the charge. He used every bit of resilience within his inner being to avoid flying into a rage at the false, but clearly, serious charge.

'Not guilty, Your Honour,' he shouted, almost at the top of his voice.

'I vehemently deny this—' he screamed, as the officers forcibly removed him and took him back to the prisoners' truck. He was then returned to his dark cell on the prison complex.

Sanjay was immediately informed of the invasion of the compound by the authorities and made a phone call straight away. He left immediately for the institute.

Back in California where it was early evening, Norman's phone rang.

'Norman, it is Sanjay from Delhi. We have a serious situation currently developing at the institute.'

'Oh dear, what's happened,' Norman asked anxiously. 'Is Robert all right?'

'The compound of the institute is being raided by the authorities. It looks like a military operation.'

'Where is Robert then?'

'He has been arrested and taken away.'

'I am on my cell phone. Please keep me updated. I am making arrangements this instant to come over.'

Norman chartered a jet and left straight for the airport. At the airport, he saw the news on the television. His bruised and battered friend was paraded through a courtroom in Delhi. He immediately contacted the American Ambassador, who was an acquaintance of his, and asked for his help, as he was still hours away. He also made another crucial phone call to ensure the safety of the kids at the institute.

A diplomatic team at the embassy was hurriedly assembled to collect information and evidence about the charges, so that Norman would have as much as he could to work on when he got there. A segment of the team left immediately to the institute where the kids were held in temporary custody.

They found the institute well secured by properly armed military men, as if it was a war camp. After some negotiations, and with the help of Sanjay, they eventually got clearance to enter. However, their movements within the building were restricted. As they walked through, they saw rooms full of scared and crying kids, who were guarded by the patrolling armed men.

They were met by an interim team set up by the office of the Governor to take over the running of the services at the institute. This team was led by someone who Sanjay immediately recognised — Mr Patel.

'Good to see you again,' said Patel to Sanjay in a hoarse voice and grinning maliciously.

'What's happened here?' asked Sanjay angrily. 'How did you get appointed to run the services of this institute? How did this all happen?'

'That is not so important now, my friend. As you know and I know, things... happen. And sometimes it happens for the best, by God's grace,' he declared rotating both his hands as he spoke and shaking his from side to side, as if he agreed with himself wholeheartedly.

'Where is Mr Lancaster?' asked Paul from the Diplomatic Corp.

'This is not my business,' Mr Patel answered. 'But I am told that he has been arrested for a serious charge.'

'What serious charge is that?' asked Sanjay.

'Well, what I have heard — I do not know this for myself — but he is a bad man. He has been molesting the young kids in the school,' said Patel.

'Nonsense!' shouted Sanjay, losing his temper.

This incensed Patel who shouted back.

'Don't worry my friend, we have solid proof. He is going to jail for life!'

No sooner than he said this, he realised the significant mistake he had made. Anger had gotten the better of him and blew the thin veil of cover, revealing his involvement in this plot.

Before Norman managed to set off on his flight, he phoned Sanjay and relayed a message to pass on to the kids. Sanjay went to every classroom with Paul and gave the students this message of hope. This was coded so as not to alert the guards or any of Patel's team. They then left and returned to the embassy. There, they tried to put together evidence to support the release of Robert.

At nine p.m., Norman arrived at the embassy and raised a petition with the courts immediately for an initial hearing on the next day, as there was serious evidence of abuse of the judicial system in this case. He was counselled by the diplomatic team and prepared his case for the following day.

He managed an hour of rest before he headed out the following morning to the court.

The hearing was done in the Magistrate's chambers. When Norman got there were already an extensive team of senior lawyers, the best in Delhi. The magistrate welcomed everyone and mentioned that he did not have much time that morning for an extensive discussion, but was willing to briefly consider the major arguments of the case.

'Your Honour, thank you for agreeing to hold this meeting today,' started the lead prosecutor. He had a full head of neatly combed black hair, but it was the sagginess of the skin on his face that was more of a true reflection of his age. He spoke with a deep British accent and with a commanding voice.

'The defendant was arrested on allegations of sexual molestation of minors at an institute for vulnerable children, which he built and runs.'

'Your Honour, I am the lead counsel for the defendant', said Norman. 'I have had the privilege of knowing the defendant on both personal and professional levels for many years and I can, without a doubt, tell you that he is not a paedophile or criminal in any form or manner.'

'We have compelling evidence to prove beyond any shadow of doubt that the defendant is guilty of the crime that he has been accused of, Your Honour,' said the barrister.

'I do not know what sort of evidence the lead prosecutor is talking about, but I would like to be privy to this because, if anyone here is guilty of anything, then it must be the Governor. We have reasons to believe that any evidence is likely to be fabricated. My client has been the victim of a set up to deny him the right to carry out his philanthropic work which he started here over a decade ago,' argued Norman.

'Your Honour, we have the testimony of one of the children, a ten-year-old who has been brutally raped and savaged by that monster!' said the prosecutor.

Norman was thrown off by this statement. This could not be right at all. He knew that this was all fabricated and that he needed to prove that this terrible crime did not happen.

'Your Honour, the lead prosecutor has mentioned the testimony of one child. If there are any more, then he should let us know.'

'Your Honour, with the testimony we hold, this is sufficient to prove that the defendant is guilty. If he has done these horrible things to one child, then it is quite likely that he has also done this to others. As is well known in situations like this, witnesses are not easily forthcoming,' argued the barrister.

'Your Honour, on the contrary to my counterpart's weak argument, I would like to say that the testimony from a single child, out of a school of 2,500 children, with regards to the accused who has an impeccably clean record from any crimes in his lifetime, I would argue that the testimony is fabricated,' said Norman.

'Objection!' screamed the prosecutor.

'Mr Fitzpatrick you cannot make accusations without evidence to substantiate them,' said the Magistrate sternly to Norman.

'You are right, Your Honour. I do not have the evidence but I am going to uncover it!' said Norman determinedly. 'I would like to request that the prosecution team provide us with the copy of the details of the testimony.'

'Okay, that's enough,' said the judge. 'The prosecution will provide copies of all items of evidence and I will consider an early trial, considering the seriousness of the charges and that this is a high-profile case'.

He dismissed both teams.

Later that day, Norman received a copy of the testimony from one of the children at the institute. It was sent to him by a fax transfer. He anxiously feasted his eyes on the content and studied every bit of detail on the report.

The following day, he was granted permission to speak to his client. He was appalled by the horrible conditions under which his friend was kept under. They sat and spoke for an hour before Norman had learnt enough to build a credible defence for the American.

The trial was scheduled for a hearing in two months, due to a large backlog of cases. Norman tried desperately to arrange another meeting with the magistrate and his counterparts to discuss a major concern. The soonest this could be arranged for was in two weeks' time.

At the hearing, Robert argued that the testimony was fabricated. He argued that the exact time and date in question, when Robert allegedly raped the child, was the night he spent outside comforting another child who desperately pleaded with him to find his mom. It was that night he played the beautiful music for Patar. Norman produced evidence of Robert's swipe card when he left the building and when he returned, together with a testimony from Patar to confirm his alibi.

Robert was then released from prison without being charged. However, in the time that he been in prison, a lot had changed. Sanjay briefed him that the licence to run the institute was retracted by the Governor and attempts were made to incarcerate all the kids. The compound has been occupied by the military. There were plans on the way to convert the institute into a prestigious college for the more privileged kids in the society.

Upon release, Robert was given a hand-delivered note from the Office of the Governor that stated that he no longer had rights to stay in the country and ordered him to leave the country within twenty-four hours. Failure to comply would result in him being deported back to the States. He asked to visit the institute, but this was not possible, as the place was heavily guarded. Robert feared for the safety and well-being of the kids which he meant so much to him. Norman assured him that there was a plan in place and that they would continue to fight the fight from America.

Chapter 26
Dances with Betrayal

Attachment inevitably leads to disappointment

As the news broke and images of a handcuffed CEO flashed across the television screens of millions of Americans, the public's image of Robert's company took on a devastating hit. Investor confidence plummeted, and carried the stock prices with it. The alarm of panic sounded. For such a strong company, this was likely to be a storm that, in all probabilities, the company could have weathered for the few weeks that it took for Robert to clear his name in the courts. However, one person saw an opportunity for himself in this storm — Hoffman.

As the news broke, he called an emergency board meeting to launch a coup. With everyone gathered into the room with a sense of anxiety and uncertainty, Hoffman asked for the door to be shut closed and for his colleagues to respect the confidentiality agreement they have all signed to not divulge any matters discussed in that room on that evening.

'Colleagues, ladies and gentleman, I have called this emergency sitting. I would like to thank you for taking the time to be here at this late hour,' he said, as he stood up and started pacing slowly around the boardroom table.

'Some time ago, I warned you all about this, the possibility of this situation developing with the CEO of this company, in this very room,' he stated, raising his voice emphatically towards the end.

'It was dismissed as nonsense at the time by some of you, but I tell you that the signs were clear then, as they were there just recently. This is the last thing that any of us would want to happen, for the interest of this great company. But sadly, we did not have the will to stop it then, which would have been the right time to act. As such, we are now faced with a situation where the CEO, who is the face of this company, has been formally arrested in a foreign land for the unspeakable crimes I specifically warned you about this before!'

The board members all bent their heads with a sense of failure and guilt of not heeding Hoffman's warning before. Hoffman, saw the weakness of his colleagues and intended to exploit it maximally, in order to manipulate them, as best as he could.

'I therefore propose that we release the current CEO of his position and role in this company in order to protect the company. We have to act now!' he demanded. 'I also propose that you elect me as your new CEO and chairman immediately, on an interim basis to guide this company through the turbulent times ahead, especially, over the next days, weeks and months. I think you would all agree that I am best placed to take on this role.'

'All in favour please raise your hands,' he instructed.

The majority of the members voted for his proposition and Hoffman was immediately installed as the new interim CEO and Chairman. This gave him sweeping powers and full control of a company, built up straw by straw, by a now imprisoned visionary.

His first act at the helm was calling an end to the board meeting. Everyone stood up and left quietly, although there were many thunderous emotional storms brewing within each of them, fed by disappointment and uncertainty. Outside the building as they emerged, there was a large crowd of reporters, accompanied by the bright lights of television cameras, desperately seeking interviews and information to feed their desperate viewers.

Hoffman gave a brief interview to update the public on the outcome of the meeting and he attempted to reassure the public in an attempt to solicit public confidence. As all the board members left, Hoffman went back into the building and spent the entire night in his office. The following morning, he sent out a message to all the board members informing them for their required presence at an emergency board meeting at 7.45 a.m.

The boardroom was full with all the members at 7.40 a.m. They all awaited the arrival their new boss. At exactly 7.45 a.m., Hoffman entered into the room with an air of authority. He appeared a bit dishevelled, unkempt and he clearly did not shave. They all looked up to him excitedly, to hear what great plans he had to take the company forward in this crisis.

'Ladies and gentlemen, I have been up throughout the night, thinking about the status of this company and how we could go forward. As you will be aware when the Stock Exchange opened just over an hour ago in New York, our stocks have depreciated dramatically following the news of the arrest of our previous CEO and Chairman in India,' Hoffman stated.

'Now I have to ask myself, was this preventable?' Hoffman went on to ask. 'Some may say no, some say maybe, but I say yes,' he said, raising his voice.

'Like I have said last night, I warned you all before that his would happen. My warning was not heeded,' the now angry Hoffman continued.

'We have now failed our investors; we have now failed our employees; we have now failed our clients all over the world, and we have failed the children that the monster has abused. Ladies and gentlemen, let's face it; look in the mirror — we have failed ourselves,' he said. 'As a result, and after much contemplation, I have decided to relieve every one of you from your duties on this board!'

Immediately there were loud voices of disappointment and shouting across the room, with everyone trying to voice their dissatisfaction all at the same time.

'You cannot do this!' one shouted. 'This is the height of deception,' shouted another.

Hoffman waited for the noises to die down before he spoke again.

'As the CEO and Chairman of this company, every one of you knows that I have the full power and authority to do this. I hope you would respect my decision.'

They all realised that he was serious about this and had the power to do exactly as he wished.

'I know that we are all in a difficult situation here, this morning. Allow me to extend an olive branch to you', he said calmly afterwards. 'I know that you have all put your lives and souls into this company, to build it up to where it was yesterday, but today it is a sinking ship. If you support my decision to liquidate the assets of the company by close of business today, each of you will receive a million dollars as a parting present,' Hoffman proposed.

'And what do you get?' one member asked.

'That is none of your business,' replied Hoffman calmly. 'Do we have a deal?'

Everyone agreed. By the next morning, the majority of the assets of the company were sold and at the end of that day the company was defunct. The company's shares were worthless and all the investors lost their financial investments. Hoffman resigned the following day, leaving no forwarding address.

The following few weeks, the IRS led an extensive investigation into the finances of the company dating back to its inception. The findings were mind blowing. They uncovered a number of anomalies over the previous ten years. The company's earnings were consistently under-reported to avoid paying large sums of taxes; there were frequent transfers of large sums of funds to the Lancaster Charity Foundation — up until a few weeks previously — that seemed to vanish into thin air, and massive sums deposited into offshore accounts under various names, all traceable back to one Robert Lancaster. This was unbelievable!

The FBI was informed and they initiated a massive investigation. All the misdemeanours seemed to point to one person, Robert Lancaster. They believed that he was using his charity work in India to deflect attention from his criminal activities. But there were still some questions which could not be satisfactorily answered. This is a gentleman who was running his charitable organisation using his own funds. In fact, he had sold his own house in LA to fund this. Why would he then siphon large quantities of money to stash in foreign countries? Surely, he would already have tapped into these resources before now. But the investigators believed that this provided him with the perfect alibi.

As Robert was cleared of the charges in India and released from prison, Norman updated him of serious troubles within the company and its impending doom. He was asked to leave India at the same time. This was obviously a politically motivated act. He was denied a chance to visit the institute which he founded and where his actions touched the lives of so many and vice versa. He no longer had any influence on their fate. Things did not look good for these kids and as hard as he had tried, it looked as if all the great work they had performed over the years was to be reversed, and the lives of the children would undoubtedly be destroyed without guidance and support.

Robert was not afforded a chance to say goodbye to his loved ones. His heart sank into darkness, knowing that he probably would never see the little boy who inspired his work here in India. He never would be able to share with him that beautiful piece of music they both loved. Hopefully he was able to impart some hope to the boy, and the others, so that no matter what and, despite the many obstacles they may have to face, they would appreciate that hope exists. His only consolation was that his work had brought him immeasurable joy and satisfaction over the years. He pledged to himself that he would spend some time in LA to sort out the problems there and work from there to legally challenge the Governor's invasion of the institute and persevere in his fight to save the children's future.

Robert was placed on flight direct to LAX. When he landed, as he entered the terminal building at the airport, there was an extensive team of men in black suits waiting to greet him. He could not recognise any of them as being his employees, and thought that there were so many changes to the company without him noticing, and that he really needed to devote more attention to it. As he approached the group, one of the gentlemen, began walking directly towards him.

'Robert Lancaster?' the gentleman asked, in a stern tone of voice.

'Yes, I am,' he replied.

To Robert's surprise, the gentleman reached into the inner pocket of his suit and withdrew a badge in his hand and displayed it to him.

'Sir, I am Special Agent Todd Morrison from the FBI Fraud Division. I regret to inform you, sir, that you are now under arrest for money laundering. You have the right to remain silent and refuse to answer questions. Anything you say may be used against you in a court of law. You have the right to consult with an attorney before speaking to the FBI and to have an attorney present during the questioning now or in the future.'

Robert was speechless at first.

'Sir, this must be some sort of mistake,' said Robert.

'No', replied the Special Agent. 'I am afraid that this is real and it's happening.'

Unfortunately, Norman did not accompany Robert on the flight as he had stayed back to sort out some urgent issues with regards to the kids, as Robert had instructed him to. Robert indicated to the men that his attorney was in India and would need to come over before he would agree to participate in any interviews with them. He was allowed to phone Norman and they agreed that Norman would come the following week.

'Sir, you do know that we would have to place you in a high security prison in the meantime.'

'Do what you have to,' Robert instructed the men. 'I do not know what you think you know, but I am clean. I have not been involved any activities which would interest you guys. I am innocent of whatever you think I have done.'

'Yes, we know. We've heard that before, once or twice', said the Agent, sarcastically.

The following week, Norman arrived and Robert was interviewed. He was given a detailed account of the charges. He denied all it as he was not aware of any foreign accounts in his name. He was consistently told over the years that all taxes were taken care of. He was shown a number of documents with his signature on them that he approved. Robert denied ever seeing those documents.

Shortly after, a trial was arranged. It was a short one. The evidence presented by the FBI were compelling and Robert did not have much of a defence, despite the herculean efforts of his good friend, attorney and confidant, Norman Fitzpatrick. He was sentenced to 133 years in prison by the magistrate, with no opportunity for an early release.

Life can change in a moment, equally through tragedy or fortune. Although the world outside may throw a hat into the ring to judge whether the modality of that change was good or bad, only through studying the big picture, that that may be determined.

Robert stood up at the counsel table as the verdict was read by the Magistrate. He was expressionless. The previous month in solitary confinement had robbed him of his emotions. He came into the court that day expecting the worse. He was preoccupied by thinking whether there was anything left that he had a burning desire to do. If there was, the joy over the last ten years or so was enough to quell the fire of desires within him.

After it was all said and done, he skimmed around the courtroom with his eyes. It was filled with journalists and cameras. He was looking for one person in particular though. He wanted to say goodbye to his son, Oscar. But unfortunately, he was not there. This tugged on a string in his heart. But, if he had learnt anything in life, you cannot control everything or everyone. Everyone has a mind of their own and one had to give others space to act how they feel appropriate at the time. Everyone dances with fate in different ways. Oscar's absence there that day did not mean that he did not exist and Robert was comforted by that knowledge, at least.

As Robert was escorted out of the courtroom, he looked up at his dear friend Norman. Their eyes fixated on one another's and Robert received a slight nod from Norman which he was desperately seeking. This was to be the last time they would see each other.

Chapter 27
Dances with Silence

Silence and reflection are enabling. They help to build inner strength

The once confident billionaire spent the first couple of years in solitary confinement in a high security prison cell. From his site of occupation, there were no avenues for communication with the world outside. For him, nothing else existed, but a room, about ten feet by ten feet with a metal door and a tiny window on the door which was closed, apart from twice a day, when it would open to allow a tray of what some would call a meal to pass through. Towards one corner of the cell there was an exposed toilet bowl and multi-coloured and multi-stained wash sink. He had no bed as such, but a dirty, worn mattress laid onto the cold concrete floor.

He did not mind his new conveniences as they were more than he expected. In his life, he had been fortunate to witness the misfortune of others. This stimulated a sense of humility in him that had become sewn in the fabric of his personality. He found himself drowning in guilt, although he not only did not know why or how he came to land into such unfortunate circumstances. For most, fate is predictable and remains fairly constant throughout a lifetime. But for Robert, fate kept moving, changing, twisting. One step forward, two steps backwards; two steps forward, one step backwards; to the left and to the right. Many moves, different outcomes. Fate was dancing with him and he managed to remain engaged, at least so far.

This final act was a blow from which he did not believe that he could have recovered from. Although he had known misfortune at various stages in his life, this was extraordinary for him, especially as he had already tasted fame and success at unprecedented levels. This made it all the more bitter for him. He had not only attracted failure and allegations of serious corruption, but he felt that he also disappointed many who believed in and depended on him for survival.

His feelings of guilt were fuelled by constant thoughts of how things could have been different had he acted differently. But how could he have chosen his dances with fate differently? He always lived a principled life, enhanced by strong ethical and moral values, respectful of other individuals and with strong purpose and determination. This steered him as he negotiated his way in life; every decision, every action. Therefore, he felt as if, despite the consequences or the circumstances, he had to own his present predicament as he had done with his previous fate.

Although it is easily done every day, it is difficult to judge the actions of individuals. Everyone is on a different point of their own journey. We all negotiate our fate differently. Each of our fates is also influenced by the actions of others. So, it is sometimes well worth to look at the broader picture and appreciate the sum total of everyone's fate, rather than that individually. This is not only more valuable, but is a better reflection of who we really are.

Had the businessman spent all his time and effort running his company, he would have possibly been in a position to change the fate of this predicament. He would have meticulously studied every detail and transaction, and discouraged the dishonesty and fraud which happened under his leadership. But, would the world have changed to provide better lives for two thousand kids who hadn't a shred of hope?

His imprisonment provided him with a chance to make peace with his inner self, through reflection and self-analysis. Slowly, he began to realise inner strength again, as the feelings of guilt and worthlessness melted and oozed away. He even started being thankful for this opportunity, as the blow of him losing his once highly successful company became far more than tolerable to him. Equally though, it could have been enough to drive him towards self-demise by suicide.

After a couple of years, he was moved out of solitary confinement and placed into a cell with metal bars, through which he could mentally participate in a world larger than a ten-by-ten room. Soon afterwards, he was allowed to have meals in a communal space with other prisoners. After sometime, he was even assigned the task to help with serving of the meals for the other inmates. Slowly, as his inner strength recovered, so to, did his sense of confidence and ambition. Not too long after, he was tasked with the role of teaching other willing inmates basic accounting skills. He used every opportunity he had to motivate his fellow prisoners in an effort to try to reform their previous ways of life, and to encourage them to see life in a different way.

In his private moments, he continued making peace with himself. He was able to overcome most regrets, but one remained at the foremost of his mind. Following the death of his wife, he felt that he had also lost his son. They had lost much of the strong emotional bond they once shared. If he had to do it all over again, this was one thing he would want to do differently. He was heartbroken that Oscar was not there as his trial, and that he did not have a final chance to make peace with him, to bid him goodbye or to tell him that he loved him very much. When he moved into his new cell, he was offered the chance to make one phone call. He called Oscar, who answered the call but immediately hung up when he heard his father's voice on the line.

Robert began writing about his life, an uncensored version that reflected the truth about the conditions and challenges that he faced and the reasons for the choices he made along the way. He intended to send this to Oscar. If after he had had a chance to read it, he still did not have much affection towards to him, maybe at least, he would understand his father better and maybe he would understand the reasons behind some of his choices along the way.

He spent two to three hours every night writing after the lights went off in the building. He used the moonlight emanating through the small window at the top of the wall of his cell as a lamp. Every time he went to the classroom to teach, he would take a few sheets of printing paper back with him to the cell. He had to write in miniscule fonts, almost microscopically, to optimise the use of his limited supply of paper.

As the years went by, this practice helped Robert immensely. He realised that there were many unresolved issues that he needed to reflect upon, but had shelved because he simply did not have the time. This helped him in his journey of making peace with himself and with his inner healing process.

After seven years, he finally completed his story. By then he had become very helpful to the administrative team and earned himself a favour. He asked for special permission to send his completed notes to his son. After review by the prison warden, this was approved, and they even paid for the postage and handling.

Over the following few years, Robert's health began declining due to an unhealthy diet, lack of regular exercise and poor medical attention. He spent more time by himself in his cell. He hoped that he could one day see Oscar, even if it was for the once. But he knew that this possibility was remote and that he was destined to live out his days in that prison.

Meanwhile, in New York, on the fifty-eighth storey of a modern office skyscraper, a package had arrived for a prominent forensic accountant at his office.

'I have a package delivered by special mail for you, sir,' said a young woman to her boss.

'Who is it from?' the man asked curiously.

'Doesn't say, but it has come from the California State Prison in Los Angeles,' she replied.

The accountant looked up sharply and collected it from his secretary.

'Thank you,' he said, with a guarded tone of voice.

'Is that all, Mr Lancaster?' she asked.

He nodded and the woman left the room. Oscar Lancaster carefully opened the package and found a file with a thick stack of papers. Each sheet was covered on both sides with minute scribbles. It did not come with a cover letter. He began reading it, and became overwhelmed. He went over and locked his door. He phoned his secretary and asked her to cancel all his appointments for the day and that he was not to be disturbed under any circumstances, for the rest of the day.

As he read the manuscript, it detailed his father's early life. Oscar was moved by the fact that his father was orphaned as an infant and he cried as he went on further and further along the rest of the pages. He realised how much he did not know about the man he had come to detest so much. He realised that he had misunderstood the kind of person his father really was, what he stood for and the reasons that he lived his life in the manner he did.

Oscar left his office late that night, unable to sleep. The events described in his father's manuscript played over and over again in his mind. Although there was not much in there to explain his alleged charges or his defence, it became obvious to Oscar that his father was not a dishonest criminal, and that he may have been set up. Oscar was determined to investigate this further.

Over the next few years, he scrutinised every financial report and the minutes of every board meeting of his father's company. A picture began emerging, involving a string of irregular activities. He needed further evidence and he went on to retrieve bank records of a few individuals who worked for the company, as well as the financial records of the Lancaster Foundation in India. He also manged to trace off shore bank accounts held by Mr Hoffman and requested transcripts through government agencies.

All the clues pointed to a criminal conspiracy by the former Head of Accounting. He stumbled upon falsified tax payments that were presented to the board. It was the work of professionals and their actions were clearly premeditated.

Once he had collected enough evidence to incriminate the true criminals, he discussed it with a colleague on the West Coast. He was a fierce and incorruptible forensic accountant who went through the evidence in detail and suggested that they should seek a legal opinion from the District Attorney for Los Angeles.

A meeting with the DA was hastily convened and the evidence presented to him. The DA, a tall man with dark hair intermingled with greys, and a flushed tired facial appearance was extremely enthusiastic about the evidence. His eyebrows elevated with curiosity and interest when he looked at the summary report prepared by Oscar.

'Mr Lancaster, I have done my research and have found that you have an impeccable reputation for honesty and competence. I would need to formally request that you pass on all the records you have in relation to this matter. I will have my experts look at them and I will get back to you in due course,' the DA said.

Months passed by and Oscar did not hear anything from the DA until late one evening, when he had a call from the secretary of the DA asking if he was free to have a chat with the DA. He thought this was a slight bit queer as he would have expected a call for an appointment to discuss the matter.

'Mr Lancaster, good-evening! I take it that you are well and all of that,' the DA started, with excitement in his voice. 'I have just come out of a meeting with the FBI. They became interested in our matter once we started perusing and studying the evidence you provided. They have allocated a lot more resources than I could ever have done and they have left no stones unturned in this matter.'

'I wasn't aware that the FBI was involved at all,' said Oscar.

'Neither did I, Mr Lancaster, until this afternoon,' said the District Attorney. 'But like I have said, I just came out of a meeting with them. Based on the evidence that they have gathered, in addition to yours, it is irrefutable that a crime had been committed. But, more importantly, your father has been jailed for a crime that he is entirely innocent of.'

Oscar went silent on the phone, reflecting on the years that his father was punished for this. His voice cracked as tears tumbled down his face in regret. He quickly wiped them away and composed himself.

'What next, sir?' he asked.

'Well, we have an appointment with the Magistrate tomorrow in his chambers, to present our case. I would like to invite you to this hearing. If the judge sees things the way I believe he is going to, then your father will be released immediately.'

This delighted the forensic accountant and he immediately made plans to fly over to LA that night.

At the hearing the following morning, the magistrate concluded, as expected, that Robert Lancaster was innocent and an order was made for the immediate release of the ex-businessman. Outside the chambers, an FBI agent approached Oscar and informed him that a sting operation was happening that second in George Town in the Grand Cayman.

'Oscar, on behalf of my Office, I would like to offer my most sincere apologies for the unwarranted imprisonment of your father,' the tall DA told Oscar, as he stretched out his arm to shake his.

'I understand, we will blame this one on the system,' Oscar said resentfully.

Oscar left the courthouse and took a taxi to the prison.

Back at the prison, it was a just the start of another day. Robert was assigned that morning to helping in the kitchen. He limped over to the peg where the aprons were and picked up one, when a tall and towering officer stood behind him and took it away.

'You are not going to need this today, or any more for that matter,' he said, in his regular deep, harsh tone of voice. Robert appeared confused. He had gone through so many ups and downs in his life to this point that he surrendered himself completely to whatever was going to hit him next.

'Follow me, Mr Lancaster,' said the prison officer.

The route they took on this early morning walk was a strange one to him, as they navigated a maze of corridors within the building. At the end of a corridor, the officer swiped his card against the device on the wall and the double doors flew open. Standing just beyond the doors was his son, Oscar!

Robert's heart bubbled with excitement to see his son, despite the cold bond they shared before. He walked briskly forward and hugged him tightly. Oscar broke down crying and hugged him tightly with a firm grip. No words were even exchanged up to this point. Behind the doors, the officer waved as they closed. Robert was confused. Oscar noticed this.

'Dad, do not worry. You are now free!' said Oscar with a juvenile strike of laughter, still with tears all over his cheeks.

'Son, I am sorry for everything,' said Robert.

"Dad, you have nothing to worry about. The world might not know it, but you are the greatest of all heroes. You have done more for the world than anyone knows.'

Robert sighed deeply.

'How is Norm?' he asked.

Oscar bent his head, and then said that he had passed on since. Robert became sad.

'He was a good man,' said Robert.

'I know,' said Oscar. 'Dad, you are coming back with me to New York. How do you feel about this?'

'Son, thank you so much, but I would very much prefer to stay here. It is warmer.'

Oscar smiled in agreement. Robert walked out of the building, a free man, that morning in stark contrast to when he entered some fifteen years before. This time there were no television cameras or reporters or millions of onlookers. He walked out a simple man, broke financially, but emotionally stronger than ever before. No longer was his life exciting enough for the world to take notice of. But at last, he was more at peace with himself than he had ever been in his life.

Oscar managed to arrange for his dad to be enrolled into a residential care home for the elderly in LA, and Robert spoke to him at least twice every day. They talked about everything, from music to astronomy. Every fortnight, Oscar came back to see him in LA and they usually went for walks. As Robert could no longer walk more than a foot or two, Oscar transported him on wheelchair — everywhere. Despite Oscar inviting him on several occasions to join him to the music hall, he always refused due to his limited mobility. The concert hall educed a pain of loss, the pain of loss that he felt for his wife and therefore, this discouraged him. However, about a year later, Oscar was pleasantly surprised when his dad accepted his invitation to a concert at the Hollywood Bowl, featuring the music of Max Bruch, Margot's favourite composer.

Chapter 28
The Final Dance

Service to humanity is the staircase to immortality

Seated at the front row of the internationally acclaimed-concert hall, the atmosphere was as light as air, very much so like that of that night many years ago, when Robert met the love of his of life for the first time. Tonight however, in contrast to that time, he was placed at the front row of the concert hall, because his mobility was limited and this was the most easily accessible area to accommodate his wheelchair. He laid back on his seat and absorbed the refreshing calm of the ambience. Seated silently next to him, was his son.

'I had forgotten what a special place this is,' said Robert to his son. 'Your mother performed on the violin to Bruch's Violin Concerto Number 1, right there on that stage. Her performance was faultless, much like her beauty and personality.'

'Is this where you two met?' asked Oscar.

'That's right! That's why this place would always be special to me.'

'Dad, then you are going to love this. Tonight, another young bright star is going to perform that very piece. He is said to be extremely talented and has become a violin maestro almost overnight. He has played in almost every major concert hall in the world including London, New York, Berlin and Vienna. He is reputed to have even played for Her Royal Highness, the Queen of England.'

'Have you heard him play before?' asked Robert.

'No, Dad, I haven't had the privilege to, but tonight we will.'

'Okay, I look forward to it, though I bet he won't be anything as great as your mom was!' chirped Robert, with a smile. 'What is his name? Have I heard of him before?'

'Peter Sneider,' replied Oscar. 'Here we go, there is a photograph of him here in the Concert Programme.'

'He is young, isn't he?' commented Robert.

At that point, the rest of the patrons entered the Hall, in a flood of activity. Whispers, low voices, the creaking of the seats, as patrons stood up to let others in and the frequent exchange of pleasantries — altogether created a melody of its own, which was in itself a prelude of the excitement to proceed. As the lights dimmed, the low hum quietened and the curtains opened to expose the stars of the evening, minus the star violinist and the conductor. The conductor that evening was, arguably, the best in the world.

The host of the evening welcomed everyone and promised a thrilling experience by the star musician, Peter Sneider. He went on to elaborate what a great honour it was to have the honour of Peter Sneider and the world-famous conductor, Sergei Ivanov, under the same roof that evening to perform together.

'Ladies and gentlemen, for the first time here at the Hollywood Bowl, I take great pleasure in welcoming the world's best conductor, Sergei Ivanov, to conduct our guest orchestra, The London Pops Orchestra.'

This was followed by loud applause from the hyped and excited audience. The conductor, a tall, elderly man, emerged from backstage wearing a black tailcoat suit. He had bushy eyebrows and a stern stare. He bowed to the audience and turned his attention, almost immediately, to the orchestra.

'Now ladies and gentlemen, I welcome on stage, the young and most talented violinist, Peter Sneider!' His voice raised in excitement as he called the musician's name out loudly.

This attracted a loud standing ovation from the audience, as the young man trotted onto the stage. He was slim and of medium height. The Viennese was of a dark complexion and flashed a warm confident smile towards his eager audience as he found his spot on the stage and sat on his seat, ready to give of his soul.

As the audience settled down and the with the commanding wave of his baton, the music of Bruch's Scottish Fantasy began. This was a treat for Robert. He laid back on his seat, closed his eyes and allowed the music to percolate through to his soul for the full length of just over thirty-three minutes. This was quickly followed by the Adagio of Bruch's Violin Concerto Number 3 in D minor, before the mid concert break.

'Oscar, can you please have a look at the programme and let me know if this talented young man is ever going to play Bruch's Violin Concerto Number 1?' asked Robert impatiently.

'Yes, Dad. In fact, this is coming up next!' quipped Oscar.

'Okay, great,' said Robert, 'I can hardly wait.'

'You like it, don't you?' teased Oscar.

'It is a fascinating piece of work, played most masterly by your mother,' replied Robert. 'Do you know the story behind that piece of music?'

'Tell me,' replied Oscar.

'Bruch revised it at least half a dozen times, you know. It took him four years,' reported Robert. 'It became so popular that in the end Bruch himself could not bear to hear it and sold it for pennies. Little did he know that that piece of music would one day become the most popular violin concerto in the world. It is not easy to play either, mind you.'

Oscar smiled warmly, as his dad always had something extra to give. By then the audience returned from their break and the performers returned on stage.

'Now, Peter Sneider is going to show us his magic. He is going to perform Bruch's Violin Concerto Number 1, under the baton of Sergei Ivanov,' announced the host.

The music started under the fiery arm movements of the conductor extraordinaire at the front of the orchestra. The first movement was sizzling and the audience was loving every note of the young man's performance. The slow movement was powerful. The brisk, but calculated arm movements, controlling the bow translated into a sublime musical performance.

As Peter started the final movement, the coordination of his hands and fingers was effortlessly faultless. At the height of his brisk, complicated solo manoeuvres, something, unheard of before, occurred. In the middle of Ivanov's passionate arm movements, Peter stopped abruptly. The brief moment of silence that followed was like a bullet to the heart of the completely astonished conductor. He energetically waved his baton, in the hope that whatever had just happened would go away and Peter would resume playing. But Peter remained motionless, as he stared fixedly into the audience.

At first it looked as if he was having a mental breakdown of some sort. By this time, the entire orchestra had stopped too. Ivanov was staring at them with fire in his eyes. He looked from side to side and concentrated his attention on the motionless star-violinist. He kept trying to kickstart the music with the movements of his baton but sadly, his efforts were initially futile. He felt completely embarrassed. Never in his illustrious career had anything like this ever happened to him.

Suddenly, Peter picked up his violin and passionately repositioned it and with his bow began playing again, much to the delight of Ivanov. His relief was short lived though, as seconds later the notes were all wrong, the melody completely different. What on earth was he doing? What was he playing? Ivanov gave a clear and firm signal for Peter to stop. But Peter kept going. The confused conductor kept turning around and signalling for everything to stop. He could not recognise that something special and powerful was happening there that evening.

Peter continued playing a tune with an unsurpassed passion that won the interest of the audience, although no one knew what it was; no one, apart from one person in the entire concert hall — Robert Lancaster. It evoked a powerful emotion like none other, it brought tears to Robert's eyes, not only to hear it played but, to hear it played so eloquently. Although it was a popular tune in a world far away, Robert knew, that of all the people there that evening, this music was meant for only him.

Peter stared at the old man seated at the front row, as tears tumbled uncontrollably down his cheeks. He stood up and walked towards the front of the stage, not missing a note.

When he got to the edge of the stage he jumped down with the violin in his possession, walked to the front of the elderly man and to the further surprise of the audience, knelt before Robert Lancaster crying uncontrollably whilst playing the beautiful tune. As Peter Sneider continued playing the tune on the violin, he was soon joined by someone else in the orchestra — someone on drums. The violin and the drum produced a compelling rendition of the popular Indian hymn from a time past, 'Jai Jagdeesha Hare.'

Robert was overcome with humility and joy, as at that moment in time, he realised the value of his work in Delhi many years ago. He then also realised that the plans he had conjured with Norman to extricate the kids to safety had worked. It was obvious that this was one of the kids from the institute in Delhi. At that moment, at the height of this emotional explosion, although the audience did not understand the reason for what was happening, they joined the violinist in honouring the man whom he was paying his utmost respect to. They all stood up in reverence to Robert.

Ivanov using his talent, coaxed the orchestra to join in with the chorus of the music in sheer support of Peter. It did not matter one bit that some of the notes were a bit off here and there; this was indeed a special moment on a grand scale. Peter just had so much he wanted to offer Robert that he kept playing and playing, with tears of love flowing from his now red and sore eyes. When he finally finished, he bowed respectfully to Robert.

'Baba, it's me Patar!' he said to Robert.

Robert was so emotionally charged with joy that he could not speak. He just sat there and cried like a baby as well.

'I am so, so overjoyed tonight to meet you, my son,' the former philanthropist said.

'I could never, ever thank you enough, Baba,' said Peter. 'I was rescued and brought up in Switzerland. I don't know how you did it, but your plan worked.'

'Did the others escape as well?' asked Robert.

'Baba, everything was kept very secretive for our protection, but I insisted to the team that I would only leave after everyone was sent away safely. So, I take it that they were all taken care of.'

'Son, you have done well. I am so proud of you. You are beyond great,' said Robert.

'Thank you so much,' said Peter.

Peter returned to the stage and walked over to the podium.

'Ladies and gentlemen, please join me in recognising the greatest hero of our time, a man I call "Baba", but whose name many of you would probably recognise, Mr Robert Lancaster.'

There was a standing ovation for the former business man. The audience remained standing, refusing to take their seats.

'I was born to an extremely poor family in India and at the age of three or four, I was homeless and lived on the streets. I had nothing; no food, no warmth, no clothes, nothing, not even a dream. This man, a then successful business came on a business trip, saw me and could not leave India without saving, not only to myself, but to about two and a half thousand, of children like me. He gave us a place to stay, the best education and everything we lacked. He gave us purpose and strength, and I would not be here today if it was not for him. He went to jail, he lost his business in the process but he did not desert us even up to the end. He put clever plans in place to make sure that whatever happened, we would be properly looked after. He is the greatest hero!'

The audience, conductor and the rest of the orchestra, already standing, looked towards Robert, and bowed to the distinguished hero amongst all heroes. They then turned their attention to Patar and bowed to him as well. The hall was then filled with applause of gratitude. They were all left humbled and inspired by the work of a true humanitarian.

Afterwards, Peter came down and chatted with Robert whilst the crowd left. He asked Oscar's permission and wheeled the old man out of the hall into the foyer. He stopped for a moment as an elegantly dressed woman approached them.

'No bodyguards tonight?' she asked teasingly.

Robert recognised the South American accent of the New Yorker, who worked with the United Nations, whom he had met many years back.

'That is a dangerous assumption,' he said to her teasingly.

He turned to Peter to introduce the stranger.

'Son, this is person who was responsible for getting you to safety when I left.'

She looked at Robert and smiled.

'Your plan worked well, Mr Lancaster.'

'Indeed,' replied Robert with a smile.

Oscar was the only other person who knew the details of the plan, as they were all detailed in the manuscript Robert wrote to him. Before that evening, he thought it was all too incredulous to be true.

That night, the world knew about Robert Lancaster's wonderful acts of human kindness and his vision to change the fate of a group of innocent and unfortunate kids that the world around them ignored. The world was now not just a better place, but one inspired by his love and kindness and his passion towards humanity. He was never going to be forgotten. Although, it was not his intention, he had stumbled onto immortality, through his many dances of fate.

Epilogue

'Surrendering to the challenges of life, one accepts death; by unconditionally accepting inner peace, one is reborn'

Life is unpredictable.

Fate is mouldable.

Destiny is a dynamic concept, irrelevant to however the moon may choose to dance with the stars. It is the outcome of the many dances you have with fate. By choosing your dances wisely, one has the power to mould one's destiny.

Robert was a true architect of planning. He saw beyond what everyone else did. He counted the true success of a plan by its resilience to survive the worst. When Robert first saw the desperate plight of Patar, he knew that there would be a whole lot of others just like that unfortunate little boy. He catered for this when he established the institute in Delhi. Even in the initial stages, he saw the need to plan for obstacles along the way and for the project to survive the worst, even if he was not there. He knew that only this way of thinking would determine the survival and success of the mission.

Robert, with the help of Norman, initially devised a system whereby the kids could be adopted by some of the experts he had hired in Delhi at the first interview. This guided his strange line of questioning at the interviews on that day. He managed to select a few suitable candidates and when they were offered the jobs, they were asked to help with this mission sometime in the future. At the request of Robert, Norman had drawn up a special agreement for the candidates selected by Robert. When they were approached by Norman, all of them agreed to it the terms and conditions of the agreement. They all agreed to adopt these unfortunate kids.

It was a blessing for Robert to accidentally bump into Anna-Maria Santiago at the hotel in LA. But, mind you, this was no accident. Anna-Maria had become very interested in the mission which she had learnt all about through the UN. She had private intelligence reports of the Governor's coup which was to follow, and wanted to place herself in a position to help. Although Robert was unaware of this at the time, he saw the potential value in having her on his side and instructed his confidant, Norman, to formulate a deal with her in the event of turmoil.

Anna-Maria was a loving young lady with no kids of own, but had devoted her life to the protection of kids internationally. When Robert was deported back to the States, Norman stayed back in Delhi to enact a plan with Anna-Maria. She arranged for the secret transfer of all of the kids to various parts of India and many other countries, to be adopted by suitable couples. This was necessary, as she became aware of the intention of the Governor to have all the kids if they had remained in Delhi. The mission to extricate the kids was carried out clandestinely and involved many personnel. Everyone knew only what they needed to and nothing more.

Anna-Maria's mission was a success, but not even she knew the where the kids were sent. It was all arranged at a higher level at the United Nations for the safety and protection of the children. From time to time she received notes about the kids. She knew that they were all looked after well and were all happy in their new environment.

Patar, meeting with the inspiration of his life, stimulated the passion in him to continue the work of his 'Baba'. He started visiting the slums around Delhi. He built a school there to teach underprivileged kids the magic of music. After about five years, he developed an orchestra. The musical theme of his orchestra was 'Jai Jagdeesha Hare', in honour of Robert Lancaster. Patar's work inspired many others after him, as the movement took on momentum internationally.

A few months after that faithful night at the concert hall, Robert left this world. He did so, in the presence of his son who had come to admire him immensely. He did so in the knowledge that he had made a difference in the world. Although he was faced with many calls from life to surrender, he never did, because he could not achieve the peace he wanted until then. Robert achieved peace with himself as he took the chance to share the song of his soul with the world. Moments before he passed on, Robert thought about the words of the swami who had travelled hundreds of miles to see him. Maybe, he was right and he did have a chance to hear Margot's music once more in this life...

Life is like a bag of marbles...

So, what is it really about? Is it possibly about how full of marbles your bag is at the end... maybe, only if the marbles were love gained. However, it is more likely that the experiences involved in filling one's bag, is probably what is more important.